Who could love Carrie Winthrop?

"I'm not going to admonish you, Carrie. I'm glad that the people trust you." He smiled as she dropped her gaze. "I hope that they will learn to trust and love me as they do you."

Carrie jerked her eyes up to his. "Love?" She spat the word out bitterly. "They don't love me, Dr. Tanner. They need me." She quickly averted her eyes so that he wouldn't see the tears that would betray the depth of her wounds. "They don't love me." Her last words were soft—barely a whisper. Keeping pace with her quickened step, Zach accompanied her to her front door.

She stopped, refusing to look at him.

He touched her cheek gently, dropping his hand when she jerked back like she'd been burned. "Don't turn me away, Carrie," he whispered. "I want to be your friend."

She stared at her front door in misery, her throat aching. Why couldn't he leave her alone? "Go away, please," she choked out, still staring straight ahead.

He acquiesced, hesitating as he reached the bottom step. "I'll be praying for you, Carrie Winthrop."

She shut her eyes as if she could block out the intensity she felt radiating from him, her feet rooted to the porch until she could no longer hear his footsteps on the well-worn path.

AMY ROGNLIE has drawn on her home in Colorado for scenes in her story that assure readers God is love and He is ever willing to forgive. Amy is a pastor's wife and mother of three young children. She loves reading and writing (of course), gardening, cooking, and crocheting. "I'm just an ordinary person whom God has blessed with some talents," Amy says. "I firmly believe that if I will use what He has given me to the best of my ability, He will bless the results."

Books by Amy Rognlie

HEARTSONG PRESENTS
HP275—Along Unfamiliar Paths

After the Flowers Fade

Amy Rognlie

Heartsong Presents

This is for all my men: My wonderful husband, Greg, and our three boys, Matthew, Nathan and Daniel. Thank you for filling my life with so much joy. I love you guys!

And as always, for my Lord and Savior, Jesus Christ, who is the Source of all joy. All the glory goes to You.

A note from the author:
I love to hear from my readers! You may correspond with me by writing: **Amy Rognlie**
Author Relations
PO Box 719
Uhrichsville, OH 44683

ISBN 1-57748-637-4

AFTER THE FLOWERS FADE

All Scripture quotations are taken from the Authorized King James Version of the Bible.

Cover illustration by Lauraine Bush.

PRINTED IN THE U.S.A.

one

Bailey, Colorado
1910

He was finally home. Zach Tanner took a deep breath of the crisp mountain air, the familiar smell opening a treasure box of memories. There was deep contentment in his heart as he made his way through the well-known streets, shuffling through the bright autumn leaves like a young boy. Pleased that the small mountain town didn't look much different than when he had left it twenty years earlier, he walked slowly, reacquainting himself with each house as if it were an old friend.

Before he knew it, he stood in front of the small gray house that he remembered vaguely from so long ago. A well-tended herb garden, already bitten with an early frost, took up almost the whole front yard. "This must be it," he murmured. Timeworn but tidy, the house fit with Zach's image of its occupant, a Miss Caroline Winthrop. He came with the best of intentions, hoping to gain the older woman's confidence. *I hope she's not too set in her ways,* he thought; then smiled, picturing himself being bossed around by a gray-haired, rough-and-tumble mountain nurse. The smile still lingering on his lips, he knocked firmly on the weather-stained door.

His smile faded as the door inched open. A young woman stood before him silently, her penetrating blue eyes blazing hostility. Zach cleared his throat. "May I please speak with Miss Caroline Winthrop?"

"I'm Carrie Winthrop." The softness of her voice belied her fierce gaze.

Zach gulped. *Surely this wasn't. . .* "Are you the nurse?"

"Look, Dr. Tanner. I know who you are, so you don't have

to beat around the bush." She glared at him. "Why don't you just say your piece and be done with it?"

Zach stared at her, his dark eyes mirroring confusion as he rubbed the back of his neck. "I think there's been some misunderstanding, Miss Winthrop," he said slowly. Glancing at her, he noted how her lips trembled in spite of the rigid stance of her body. Hoping to put her at ease, he lowered his voice, using his best bedside manner. "I am not sure what you've been told, but I'm not a threat to you."

She watched him warily as he extended his hand to her.

"Could we start over, please?" he asked.

Putting out her hand with some reluctance, she clasped his for an instant. Long enough for him to feel the roughness of her work-hardened skin. She jerked her hand away, and only the buzzing of the cicadas in the nearby oak tree filled a long moment as Jach gathered his thoughts. Why did he suddenly feel like an intruder.

Apparently she had no intention of inviting him in. He shrugged inwardly, leaning against the ornate porch railing. Still she stood framed in the doorway, grasping the screen door as if it would shield her from his presence.

She looks like a cornered animal, Zach thought. He cleared his throat. "I assume since you know who I am, you also know that I've come to set up a practice here in Bailey," he began carefully.

"Yes."

She's not going to make this easy for me. Zach wondered at her austere appearance. He couldn't help noticing how her beautiful complexion was accentuated by the drab coloring of her dress. Her hair was pulled back into a ridiculously tight bun, but what he could see of it reminded him of a shiny copper penny. Just as he began wondering what could bring a smile to those frosty blue eyes, the small frown beginning between her eyebrows warned him that he'd better stop his perusal right then. He cleared his throat.

"Well, I thought that since we're going to be partners of

sorts, that I would. . ." His voice trailed off at the look on her face.

She was staring at him now, her eyes wide. "What do you mean, partners?"

"Well, I. . ." Suddenly he knew. Stifling the impulse to laugh at his own stupidity, he crossed over to where she stood.

He hadn't realized how small she was until he stood close to her. He tilted his head, pretending not to notice the way her knuckles had tightened on the door handle as he approached. "You thought I was going to try to run you off, didn't you?" He saw the answer reflected in the lake-blue depths before her gaze fell to the floor.

Ducking his head so he could see her eyes again, he sucked in his breath as he saw the anguish written there.

"Ah, don't be upset," he breathed. "I'm not here to be in competition with you. I was hoping we could work together."

She swallowed hard. All the hostility drained away, apparently taking her bravado with it. "I'm not a real nurse, I mean, I didn't go to school; I. . ." Her voice deserted her.

"Shh." He silenced her gently. "I know that you're a good nurse, Miss Winthrop. It doesn't matter to me that you got your education from experience. In fact, that's probably even better." He smiled down at her. "Now if we're going to work together, I would like it very much if you would call me Zach."

She cocked an eyebrow at him.

Taking her silence as assent, he flashed her another grin. "You know, when I first heard your name, I expected someone much older." He swept her with an appreciative glance. "Carrie definitely fits you better than Caroline." He watched in dismay as her eyes shuttered and her tolerant manner disappeared.

"Yes. Well, thank you for stopping by, Dr. Tanner," she said stiffly.

Zach wasn't sure what he had done to cause her reaction,

but he took the hint and stepped away from her. "I'll see you again soon, Carrie," he said.

❧

Zach paused just out of sight of her house. Looking back over his shoulder, he could see the smoke rising from her chimney, adding a tang of its own to the fragrant fall air. Shaking his head, he turned to go. That certainly wasn't what he had expected. Could he work with someone so. . .rigid? With a pang, he recalled the look on her face as she had waited for him to speak, almost as if she was expecting him to wound her. The haunted look in her expressive eyes, the ill-fitting clothing and too-severe hairstyle confirmed his sudden suspicion that she had been badly hurt in the past. But by whom or what?

Determined to find some answers, he strode purposefully into the small church that he knew as well as his own home. The musty smell of old hymnals and ancient pews greeted him as the white-haired minister engulfed him in a bear hug. "Good to have you home, Zach! Or should I say Dr. Tanner?"

Zach grinned at the man he had known since childhood. "Zach is just fine, Pastor Dan." A look of understanding passed between the two men and they both chuckled.

"So, what brings you to my office on a beautiful morning like this?" Pastor Dan Peterson smiled at the young man.

"I couldn't wait until Sunday to shake your hand," Zach teased as he grabbed the man in a brief bear hug. Sobering then, he looked at the pastor seriously. "I just met Carrie Winthrop."

A knowing look spread over the older man's face. "Ah, Zach. You don't waste any time getting down to business, do you?"

Zach eyed him questioningly.

"Carrie Winthrop." The pastor sighed, shaking his head. "What did you make of her?"

Zach shrugged. "She was. . .prickly."

Pastor Dan roared with laughter. "That's an apt description, if I ever heard one." He chuckled some more. "You didn't get on too well with her then, I take it?" The older man peered at Zach, more anxiousness revealed in his eyes than his laughter had implied.

"Well, once I explained that I was friend, not foe, we didn't do so bad." Zach shook his head, recalling the fire in her blue eyes. "She actually thought I was going to be in competition with her, and that I had come to throw down the gauntlet."

"But you didn't?"

"Didn't what?" Zach raised his eyebrows at the elderly minister.

"You didn't challenge her?"

Zach was astounded. "Of course not, Dan. You ought to know me better than that!"

"I was hoping I knew you that well." Pastor Dan relaxed back in his chair, blowing out a relieved sigh. "So did she agree to work with you?"

Zach stared past the older man. "I guess so," he said finally. Recalling Carrie's abrupt change in manner at the end of their conversation, he shrugged. "Not really."

Pastor Dan smiled at the look on Zach's face. "She's a hard one to read, Son." He patted a chair. "Have a seat and I'll fill you in on what I know. Maybe you can break through the barriers she has built. God knows Louisa and I have tried, but. . ."

Half an hour later, Zach had a new perspective on the young nurse. "What a hard thing for her to bear," he mused, almost to himself.

"Yes, it was, and continues to be very hard for Carrie. She's a strong young woman, but I'm afraid she's headed down the wrong path."

"In what way?"

Pastor Dan stood up and walked to the window. When he turned back around to face the young doctor, his eyes were thoughtful. "She's allowing this to make her a bitter, fearful woman." He stared at Zach. "One can't go down that path very long before it starts wreaking havoc in one's soul."

"I know, Pastor Dan. I know all too well." Zach's compassionate heart ached for the young woman. "Pray that God will be able to use me to draw her to Him, Dan," he whispered as he rose to leave.

"I will, son. He does work in mysterious ways, doesn't He?" The aged minister and the young doctor shared a hopeful smile.

≥≈

Back at Mrs. Granger's boardinghouse hours later, Zach laid his Bible down gently on the bedside table and blew out the candle. He lay staring at the ceiling for long moments, but sleep would not come. Deliberately, he quieted his racing thoughts until he could hear the familiar night sounds of his beloved town. Smiling as he heard the crickets and the bullfrogs blend into a late-summer symphony, he closed his eyes.

He was a boy again, standing on the bank of Larson's Pond. He could see the rippling trail left behind by a slow-swimming box turtle, could smell the warm mud as it oozed between his bare toes. He set his schoolbooks down, determined to catch that big blue racer he had seen yesterday. . .

"Zach! Zachary Tanner!" He pulled his shoes on guiltily. How many times had Mama told him not to be late for supper? Grabbing his books, he hurried home to Mama's forgiving smile and a hot supper. Then came the best time of the day. Zach handed Papa the large family Bible, then clambered up onto his lap.

Snuggled securely in Papa's strong arms, Zach would wait in anticipation. Papa would slowly pull out his glasses and clear his throat. Then, reverently, he would open the Bible and begin to read. Zach loved to hear the rumble of Papa's voice as he read from the precious Book. Many nights the small boy would fall asleep as his father read, the Word of God sinking deep into his impressionable young soul.

But then came the day that would change eight-year-old Zach Tanner's life forever. "We have to move away from here, Zach," his mother had told him gently.

"But why, Mama?"

"We'll explain it to you when you're older, son. It's too much for a young lad to understand right now," Papa said firmly, lovingly. "Everything will be fine, Zach. You'll see."

But everything wasn't fine. They moved to Denver City where there were no ponds, no friendly townsfolk who knew him by name, no crickets chirping at night. Zach adjusted slowly, but his heart remained in his beloved mountain home. Mama wasn't happy here, either. Sometimes he could hear her pleading with Papa at night when they thought he was sleeping.

". . .seems like you're running away, Charles."

"I'm not a coward, May. I just don't want you and Zach to have to bear the brunt of something I did."

"But you didn't. . . ."

☙

Zach woke with a start, realizing he was in bed in Mrs. Granger's boardinghouse. He sighed. The same old dream. Why couldn't he put it to rest? Maybe being back here in Bailey had touched off the memories again. Lying back down, he let his thoughts roam again, this time to the day he had announced his intentions to his aging parents.

"I've decided to set up practice in Bailey," he had said cautiously.

Mama's eyes glittered with tears and she nodded her head with vigor.

"We're happy for you, son," Charles had said, speaking for himself and his wife, who could not speak for herself anymore.

Mama's suffering was what had prompted young Zach to go into the medical profession in the first place. "I'll come visit you often," he promised. "It's not that far away."

His father's firm handshake and words of encouragement were imprinted deeply on Zach's heart. "God go with you, son," Charles had said the day Zach left. Charles had always called him son, since the day he had married Zach's widowed mother. *A man never had a better father,* Zach thought affectionately.

He caressed the cover of the Bible that his parents had given him upon graduation from the university. It was his most prized possession. He picked it up reverently, the faint moonlight just bright enough for him to make out the words that had been lovingly inscribed on the front page. *The grass withereth, the flower fadeth: but the word of our God shall stand forever.* As always, the Scripture brought deep peace to his heart. No matter what happened, God's word was true. Clutching the Bible to his chest, Zach breathed a quiet prayer of thanksgiving before slipping into a dreamless sleep.

two

Not far from where Zach lay sleeping peacefully, Carrie stood at her window, wide awake. "What am I going to do?" she asked herself out loud. She wouldn't have admitted it to anyone, least of all herself, but she was shaken to the core by Dr. Zach Tanner. *I never knew that a man could be so gentle. . .so sensitive. . . .* She shook herself mentally.

Life had been going along just fine, until *he* came. She gazed at the spot where the boyish-looking doctor had stood just hours ago. A hint of his cologne clung to her hand, and she took a deep breath, trying to dispel the sudden melancholy that descended upon her. Mindlessly fingering the edge of the lacy curtain, she recalled the kind light that shone in his dark eyes. She pictured his warm brown eyes, his gentle smile. . . *Why did you have to come now, Zach Tanner? Things were finally starting to work out for me here.* Carrie leaned her head against the cold window pane. *Oh, Grandma Esther. How I wish you were still here.*

The pain in Carrie's heart was still sharp. Grandma Esther had practically raised Carrie, taking her in when the young girl's mother had died. But Grandma Esther herself had died nearly a year ago, leaving Carrie with the small house, a wealth of herbal healing skills, and a heart full of memories. "Don't be afraid to love and be loved, Carrie," Esther had whispered. "It's worth the heartache."

The words had rung in Carrie's mind ever since. *Don't be afraid. . . . Don't be afraid to love. . . . But I am afraid*, she cried. Shaking her head to clear the troublesome thoughts from her mind, she sighed as she freed her hair from the bun that had held it captive all day. Maybe she would just cut off the whole mess one of these days. Who would care anyway?

13

She closed her eyes as she kneaded her aching head with strong fingers. Finally picking up the brush, she stroked the coppery strands until they shone, then carefully began braiding. Her fingers stopped midway through as she recalled the appreciative look she had seen in Dr. Tanner's eyes; the look that had changed to bewilderment when she had dismissed him so abruptly. *You did the right thing,* she assured herself. *He would never understand.*

She stood up in disgust. *Get ahold of yourself, Carrie Winthrop,* she commanded herself. *You know that no man can be trusted, even if he does seem sincere.* Grimly, she blew out the candle and climbed into her cold bed. She wasn't happy, but at least she was safe.

❧

Hours later, she was jerked from a fitful sleep by an insistent pounding on her door. "Carrie! Carrie Winthrop!"

Recognizing Jeb Johnson's frantic voice, she hurriedly pulled on the first dress she laid her hand on. "I'll be right there, Jeb," she called.

She grabbed her packed bag, opening the door to join Jeb who was already halfway down the street. Smiling to herself in the predawn light, she hurried after the anxious man. *He won't be quite so worked up once he realizes it will be hours before the baby is born.* She laughed softly. Delivering babies was one of her favorite duties.

The Johnson house was ablaze with light and Mary Ellen was further along in her labor than Carrie had anticipated. Jeb hovered over his wife, awkwardly patting her shoulder as another contraction peaked. He glanced up at Carrie, something akin to terror glowing in his eyes.

Carrie took in the situation in a swift glance. Motioning to Jeb, she led him into the kitchen and set a teakettle on to heat.

"Mary Ellen is going to be just fine," she told him firmly. "But you're not any help to her by being afraid." She looked the huge man in the eye. "If you want to help her, sit next to her and hold her hand. Let her feel your strength."

Jeb nodded. "How long will it be?"

Carrie shrugged. "Another hour, maybe. Can you do it?"

Jeb nodded.

"Come on, then. We've got work to do."

Concentrating on her patient, Carrie was unaware that Zach had slipped into the room. Only when Carrie triumphantly handed a squirming baby girl to the proud father did she notice Zach standing in the doorway with the teakettle and cup.

"Why, Dr. Tanner!" She had completely forgotten his existence until that moment. What was he doing here, anyway? *We'll just see how nice he is now that I was the one called to deliver this baby,* she thought. Drawing herself up and looking him in the eye as she took the teakettle from him, her mouth dropped open when he smiled at her warmly.

Turning to the new parents, he exclaimed, "Congratulations, Mr. and Mrs. Johnson. I hope I'm not intruding." Out of the corner of his eye, he saw Carrie raise her eyebrows. "I was headed to Larson's Pond to try my hand at fishing when I saw your door open and thought perhaps I could be of some assistance."

"Thanks, Doc." Jeb grinned at his wife, while Zach turned to beam at Carrie.

"Good work, Carrie! I've never seen it done better."

She closed her mouth with a snap, dropping her gaze. "Thank you," she murmured. She held the steaming cup of tea to Mary Ellen's lips, trying to hide her confusion. Suddenly needing to get out of Zach's presence, she gave a few words of instruction to Jeb as she repacked her bag, kissed Mary Ellen's forehead, then made a hasty exit.

Crunching through the crisp leaves as she wearily made her way home, she failed to hear Zach until he was walking beside her. She glanced at him out of the corner of her eye, growing increasingly self-conscious as she felt him studying her. She shifted her soiled apron to her other hand in a nervous gesture, realizing as she did so that she wore the same dress she had had on yesterday. Of course, she wasn't out to impress him, but. . .

"What kind of tea was that that you gave her to drink?"

The tone in his voice made her look up. Maybe he was going to lecture her after all. "Catnip tea. Eases the after-pains," she muttered.

He put out a placating hand, warding off the defensiveness in her eyes. "I'm not going to admonish you, Carrie. I'm glad that the people trust you." He smiled as she dropped her gaze. "I hope that they will learn to trust and love me as they do you."

Carrie jerked her eyes up to his. "Love?" She spat the word out bitterly. "They don't love me, Dr. Tanner. They need me." She quickly averted her eyes so that he wouldn't see the tears that would betray the depth of her wounds. "They don't love me." Her last words were soft—barely a whisper. Keeping pace with her quickened step, Zach accompanied her to her front door.

She stopped, refusing to look at him.

He touched her cheek gently, dropping his hand when she jerked back like she'd been burned. "Don't turn me away, Carrie," he whispered. "I want to be your friend."

She stared at her front door in misery, her throat aching. Why couldn't he leave her alone? "Go away, please," she choked out, still staring straight ahead.

He acquiesced, hesitating as he reached the bottom step. "I'll be praying for you, Carrie Winthrop."

She shut her eyes as if she could block out the intensity she felt radiating from him, her feet rooted to the porch until she could no longer hear his footsteps on the well-worn path. Finally summoning the strength to move, she opened the door, closing it firmly as she entered the silent house. Drained, she sank into the nearest chair.

How could a morning that started off so beautifully end like this? A brief smile flitted across her lips as she relived the glorious event she had witnessed. A new baby! Carrie could almost believe in a God of love when she beheld the miracle of birth. Almost, but not quite. As soon as she handed the baby over to the waiting mother, Carrie's arms were empty and cold once again. The aching feeling in her breast would return, knowing that this was a joy she would never experience for herself. No man would ever want her.

She jumped up from her chair, unwilling to indulge in self-pity. Stoking up the fire, she set a fresh kettle of water on the burner. Whipping off her stained dress, she slipped into a clean one. She went to work cleaning her instruments, fighting to erase all thoughts from her mind, but Zach's words rang over and over again. *I hope that they will learn to trust and love me as they do you.*

She laughed scornfully. What kind of man was Zach Tanner anyway? Surely he knew her whole sordid story—everyone in Bailey knew about Carrie Winthrop. What was his game? She wrinkled her brow. There had to be a reason that he was being so nice... *Perhaps he is just trying a different tack than all the rest,* she mused.

"Well, it's not going to work, Dr. Tanner," she said out loud. She pictured his gentle eyes and heard again his kind words, and sighed. It would be so easy to hate him like all the others—if only he weren't so nice. . . .

three

Zach stood on the bank of Larson's Pond, idly skipping stones across the glassy surface. He sniffed the air appreciatively, extremely pleased that all was the same as he remembered it. Sitting down on the grassy bank, he waited quietly for several minutes. His patience was soon rewarded as a family of wood ducks waddled out from the underbrush. Lying back in contentment, he studied the clouds, his thoughts drifting as lazily as the huge puffs of white cotton in the sky. It felt so good to be home! His last summer here had been the best. . .

"Zachary Tanner! You take that thing right back to the pond!" Mama's voice was stern.

"Aw, Mama. Can't I keep him for a pet?"

"Zach!"

He sorrowfully closed the lid of his dinner pail. "Come on, Joey. We'd better take him back."

Zach laughed out loud. Mama never had forgiven him for bringing a muskrat home in his dinner pail. *She was pretty tolerant of frogs, though,* he thought affectionately. He grew pensive as he reflected on the past. *What would my life have been like if we hadn't moved from here?* He gazed out across the calm water, then sighed. It wouldn't do any good to dwell on the past. He stood up slowly, reluctant to leave. A huge flock of geese heading south serenaded him as he took the long way around the pond. He stopped often to examine a flower or leaf, exulting in the beauty around him, yet feeling the melancholy lingering in his soul.

Carrie would like it here. The thought was so unexpected, he stopped in his tracks. *Where did that come from?* he wondered. He pictured the lonely young woman standing beside

him in the brush, her face lit with a smile as she bent to sniff
the delicate scent of the wandlilies that grew abundantly
around the pond. He shook his head, amused with his over-
active imagination. *Carrie Winthrop probably wishes she
would never see me again, much less take a stroll around
Larson's Pond with me.*

Yet the thought persisted, and though Zach pushed it away
time and again, he finally gave in. *Father, You're the Great
Physician. I'm just a country doctor. If it's Your will for me to
help heal her wounds, I need Your wisdom. Please show me
the way, and soften her heart. . .*

੨੩

The busy autumn days flew by. Zach spent his time visiting
the townspeople, getting reacquainted with their placid life-
style. He ran into Carrie occasionally as she went about her
business. Most of the people of the town still called for her
when they were in need of medical attention, and though he
didn't begrudge her the trust she had earned, Zach longed to
make a meaningful contribution to the community as well. It
was just by chance that he had seen her at the Johnsons' the
morning Mary Ellen's baby was born.

Frustrated by the town's seeming lack of interest in its new
doctor, Zach spent more and more time at the pond, thinking
and praying. He was in his favorite spot on the bank, leaning
against the trunk of a towering oak. He had just thrown his
fishing line in again and was watching it bob slowly, when a
movement across the pond caught his eye. Hoping it was the
doe and her fawn he had seen earlier, he froze. He gazed at
the spot intently, surprised when he saw Carrie slip through
the underbrush. Fascinated, he watched as she slipped off her
shoes and waded into the clear water. The look on her face
was the closest thing to happiness he had ever seen there.

Suddenly feeling guilty for staring at her, he dropped his
eyes to his fishing pole. *I can't get up and leave without her
seeing me,* he thought, not wanting to embarrass her. He sat
motionless, concentrating on looking anywhere else except at

Carrie. It didn't work. His eyes were drawn continually to the fiery brilliance of her hair, the look of almost-peace on her face. He wondered fleetingly what she would look like in a becoming dress, her glorious hair hanging loose. Abruptly reining in his thoughts, he picked up the medical book he had brought with him.

Tiny splashing sounds invited him to look up, but he kept his eyes steadfastly on the page. Finally allowing himself a brief glance, he realized she was gone. He rose slowly, walking back to the boardinghouse deep in thought. *So, Miss Winthrop does have some bits of happiness in her life after all.* Zach had begun to wonder if she ever did anything besides work. He never saw her in town unless she was tending to a patient. Most other girls her age spent as much time in town as they could, openly vying for the attention of the available men; himself included, he thought ruefully. Just yesterday Annabelle Parker had stuck to him like a cocklebur as he tried to go about his business. Zach gritted his teeth even now as he recalled her sugary-sweet voice and clinging hands. He sincerely hoped she wouldn't be at the Harvest Festival this weekend.

❧

The Harvest Festival was already in full swing when Zach arrived. He stood for a moment watching the crowd, smiling in fond remembrance as he watched the small boys and girls darting here and there, shouting with glee.

"Yoo-hoo, Dr. Tanner! We're over here!"

Zach grimaced as he heard Annabelle's voice over the crowd. Pretending not to notice her frantic waving, he deliberately turned in the opposite direction. Spotting Pastor Dan, he made a beeline for his elderly friend. He pumped the older man's hand enthusiastically, then turned to the minister's wife.

"How are you, Sister Louisa?" He asked heartily, using the title of respect that most of the townspeople used for the motherly woman. Out of the corner of his eye, Zach noticed Annabelle marching toward him, her nostrils flared in indignation. "Please, Sister Louisa! Can't you help me?"

Zach darted a meaningful look at Annabelle.

Sister Louisa appraised the situation in a glance, her eyes taking on a slight twinkle as she stepped out quickly from behind the long serving table. "How good of you to come help serve, Annabelle!" Sister Louisa beamed at the young woman. "I have an extra apron if you'd like, dear. Would you prefer to serve the pie or the cider?"

"But I. . ." Annabelle's voice faded as Zach and the reverend casually wandered off.

Pastor Dan laughed out loud. "It would do that pampered young lady good to do a little serving of others for a change."

Zach sent Sister Louisa a grateful smile over his shoulder, chuckling when she waggled her finger at him. "You've got yourself a fine women there, Pastor Dan."

❧

Carrie stood glaring at her reflection in the mirror. She pinned her bun in place more securely, irked that some of the coppery tendrils insisted on pulling loose to curl around her face. For days now, she had been regretting the promise she had made to Pastor Dan. After all, who would really notice if Carrie Winthrop was at the Harvest Festival or not? Slipping on her shoes, she glanced in the mirror one last time. *I'll only stay a few minutes,* she promised her scowling image. *I told Pastor Dan that I would come, but I don't have to stay.*

Setting out resolutely, she refused to let herself think of times past. Nevertheless, her steps slowed as she neared the crowded church grounds. Her heart began pounding furiously; her hands poured sweat. *Stop being silly,* she admonished herself. *No one can hurt you.* Forcing herself to go the last few feet, she sighed in relief as she spotted Sister Louisa standing by the dessert table. Taking a deep breath, she plunged into the throng, making her way almost frantically to where the pastor's wife stood chatting.

Sister Louisa enfolded Carrie in a warm embrace, her concern evident on her lined face. Taking in Carrie's pale complexion and wide eyes, Louisa turned to her companion.

"Excuse us for a moment please, Kate." Leading Carrie into the dim quietness of the church, Louisa looked lovingly into the girl's eyes. "Ah, Carrie. Is it still so hard, child?"

At Carrie's almost imperceptible nod, Louisa took her in her arms once again, her lips moving in whispered prayer.

Carrie straightened slowly. "I'm sorry, Sister Louisa," she whispered. "I tried. . . ."

"I know, child. I know." Louisa framed Carrie's face in her hands. "God is the only One who can give you freedom from this, Carrie."

Carrie looked away. "I need to go home, Louisa."

Louisa's face saddened; but she sighed in acquiescence. "I'll get the pastor to walk you home, dear."

Carrie nodded wearily, too spent to argue. Following Louisa out of the church, she stood silently watching the festivities, hoping no one would notice her. Spotting Dr. Tanner, she shrank deeper into the shadow of the church. She felt sure he must have seen her that day at Larson's Pond, even though his nose had been buried in a book when she had noticed him sitting on the bank. She had beat a hasty retreat as soon as she realized she was not alone, but her cheeks still turned rosy at the thought of Dr. Tanner seeing her wading in the pond.

Lost in thought, she started violently as one of the town's young men sauntered by. An ugly expression on his face, he let his gaze roam over Carrie boldly. "Hello, Sharayah," he sneered.

Carrie jerked as if she'd been slapped. She turned to run, but his mocking voice followed her. "Saw ya down at the pond with the doctor. Guess yer jest showin' yer true colors, ain't ya?"

※

Zach found her behind the church, retching violently. He had been surprised and pleased when he saw her arrive at the festival. He hadn't thought she would come. Making his way to where she stood with Sister Louisa, he was stopped repeatedly to answer a question or listen to a joke. He kept track of her out of the corner of his eye, smiling and nodding as he worked his way through the crowd. Finally reaching the spot where he had last seen her, he turned in a slow circle until he saw the hem of her skirt disappear behind the church.

Now as he placed a cool hand on her forehead, he kicked himself for not getting to her sooner. His first impulse was to gather her in his arms, but he knew she would push him away—or worse, she might try to fight him. Sending up a quick prayer for wisdom, he guided the weeping girl to a nearby stump. She didn't resist as he gently seated her. But catching a glimpse of her eyes as she accepted the handkerchief he pressed into her hand, a cold chill coursed through him. Her eyes were glazed with fear, her tearing sobs subsiding to low moans. She was going into shock. He left her for only a moment to motion to Pastor Dan.

The pastor and his wife came on the run, Louisa pulling Carrie to her immediately. "What happened, Zach?" Dan whispered.

Zach shrugged. "I don't know. I saw her just as she disappeared behind the church. By the time I caught up to her, she was like this. I'm afraid she's going into shock."

"We've got to get her to bed, Dan." Louisa's voice was firm, though worry was evident in her eyes.

The men nodded. Zach lifted Carrie carefully, glad that her eyes were closed. He was shocked at how little she weighed.

Louisa saw his look. "She doesn't care about herself, Zach. She eats next to nothing."

By mutual consent, Zach bore Carrie's now-limp form to the pastor's house. Laying her on the bed, Zach looked up thoughtfully. "She needs to be examined to make sure that nothing is wrong physically." He frowned. "If I do it, she will never look at me again, much less work with me. Louisa, if I tell you what to do, could you do it?"

"Certainly, Zach." Louisa smoothed Carrie's hair back. "You're going to be fine now, little one. No one will hurt you."

"No, no! Don't touch me!" Carrie struggled wildly against

the hands that ministered to her. "Stay away from me. . . ." Her screams quieted as a voice penetrated her fear-stricken mind. A soft voice. . .a woman's voice. . . .

❧

Louisa continued to apply the cold compresses, tears streaming down her face. She spoke to Carrie in low, soothing tones, her whisper-soft prayers intermingling with her crooning.

Zach stood listening just outside the open door, his heart breaking. How could men's hearts be so evil? He had heard of such abuse, but to see the end result of it manifest so plainly was a shock to his sensitive spirit. Motioning to Louisa, he waited to speak until he was sure Carrie wouldn't hear his voice. "Has the fever come down at all, Sister Louisa?"

She shook her head wearily. "I don't think so, Zach. God is our only hope now to pull her through."

Zach rubbed the back of his neck in frustration. Fearing that a setback would occur if Carrie awoke to find him in her room, he had forced himself to let Louisa care for Carrie exclusively. He sighed deeply. "God may be our only hope, Louisa, but He's a mighty God."

Louisa smiled gratefully. "I know He is, Zach. Thank you for reminding me."

Pastor Dan touched his wife's shoulder gently. "You need to rest, dear. Zach and I will call you if you're needed."

The two men stared at each other as Louisa took one last peek at the patient. "We're not fighting a physical battle here, Zach." The pastor's face was serious. "Carrie's spirit has been wounded very deeply."

Zach nodded his agreement. Clasping hands, the young doctor and the elderly minister presented their heartfelt petitions before the throne of God. Even as they prayed, the bands of fear began to loosen. . . .

❧

Carrie woke slowly, feeling as though she had been trapped underwater in a murky, dark place. She took a deep breath, and some of the blackness dissolved, allowing her to open her eyes. Closing them again quickly against the sun that poured in through the window, she lay still, considering. Where was she? Opening her eyes again cautiously, she gradually took in the frilled organdy curtains; the crocheted coverlet; the rose-covered china pitcher and bowl. . . . *Ah. I'm in Pastor Dan and Sister Louisa's house.* She closed her eyes in contentment, hardly aware that the cloud of fear that tormented her had almost completely dissipated.

Louisa flew into the room, finding the two men still on their knees. "The fever has broken! She's sleeping naturally!"

Zach jumped to his feet, tears still marking his face. "Thank God!" he whispered. "Thank You, Father!"

❧

Days later, Carrie sat up in bed, staring out the window. She had reluctantly agreed to see Zach when Louisa explained how concerned he had been for her.

"Don't be afraid of Dr. Tanner, Carrie," Louisa had said. "He has a good heart."

Carrie patted her hair nervously. She had insisted that Louisa pin it up for her before Zach arrived, but somehow it didn't feel right. She folded her hands tightly, hoping he wouldn't notice how badly they were trembling. *He has a good heart.* Louisa's words echoed in her mind as a soft knock sounded on the door.

Louisa entered followed by a beaming Dr. Tanner. He carried a small bouquet of wildflowers, which he handed to Carrie. "I thought you would like these."

She caught her breath at their delicate beauty. *Where had he found fairyslippers blooming at this time of year?* Burying her nose in the flowers, Carrie smiled hesitantly. "Thank you," she whispered.

"They reminded me of you," he said softly. "How are you feeling?"

She was afraid she might not be able to speak above the sudden thundering of her heart, but the genuine kindness in his eyes made her respond. "Better, thank you." She looked away for a moment, gathering her thoughts. What was wrong with her today? "I—Louisa said you prayed for me."

"I told you I would, Carrie," he reminded her, his tone gentle. "Don't you remember?"

Remember? How could she forget? Those last words he had spoken to her the day she had delivered Mary Ellen's baby were burned in her memory forever. *I'll be praying for you. . . .* "Thank you for letting Louisa care for me." She looked at him directly then, willing him to understand that she was thanking him for more than she had put into words.

Zach nodded. Apparently not wanting to make her uncomfortable by staying too long, he got to his feet. "I'm so thankful you're feeling better, Carrie. May I stop by again in a few days?"

She nodded, allowing herself a tiny smile in his direction.

He smiled at her in return then left the room quietly, closing the door behind him.

Carrie heaved a huge sigh of relief. *That wasn't so bad,* she admitted to herself. *Maybe Louisa was right.* Dr. Tanner did seem to have a good heart—though something was definitely wrong with hers! Why did she feel so. . .fluttery whenever he got that look in his eye? No doubt she still needed some extra rest, she decided.

She sniffed the flowers again appreciatively, then wrinkled her brow as she eased herself back against the headboard. If only she could figure out how he fit into this whole situation. Louisa had told her that Dr. Tanner had found her behind the church and had carried her to the house. Her face flamed at the thought of him seeing her in such a state. *Good grief, Carrie,* she scolded herself. *Dr. Tanner doesn't care what you look like.*

But why was I behind the church in the first place? Her mind puzzled over this for many minutes, coming up blank like every time before. *I remember waiting in front of the church for Pastor Dan. . . .* She shook her head. She just couldn't recall anything that happened after that until she woke up here at Pastor Dan's house. Why did she keep thinking that Dr. Tanner was involved somehow?

As she drifted into a troubled sleep, Carrie's mind continued to work. Half-formed images filled her dreams. Wildflowers. . . shadows. . .rippling water. . . "Yer jest showin' yer true colors. . ."

Carrie jerked awake. That was it! Clarence Yeakley had called her that despised name, accusing her of. . .of. . . She couldn't think it. Burying her face in the pillow, she wept until there were no more tears.

Louisa found her that way and gently coaxed the story out of her. "Carrie, you've got to forget about what people say or think. What does it matter that you and Dr. Tanner happened to be at the pond at the same time? Neither of you did anything wrong; and for you to be so bothered by a false accusation is foolishness. You did nothing wrong."

"But don't you see, Sister Louisa? Everyone thinks I'm the same as my mother. Why can't they accept me for who I am?" Tears filled Carrie's eyes again. "I know no man will ever want to marry me, but why can't I at least be respected?"

Louisa stared at her in consternation. "Carrie, do you really believe that any man who truly loved you would hold it against you that you were abused as a child? That wasn't your fault, honey."

Carrie dropped her gaze. "No one would ever love me that much, Louisa. In everyone's eyes I'm just as guilty as if I had actually wanted it to happen."

Louisa framed Carrie's face in her hands, forcing the younger woman to meet her gaze. "*I* love you that much, Carrie. And God does, too. In fact, He loves you even more than that; so much that He sent His Son to die for you." She smoothed Carrie's hair back gently. "Let Him love you, Carrie."

Carrie shook her head sadly. "I wish I could believe that He loves me, Sister Louisa. But I just don't see how. . ." Her voice trailed off. In her mind's eye, she could see a small red-haired girl cowering under the bed. She covered her ears with her hands, trying to block out the ugly noises from the next room. Only after she heard the sound of heavy boots tramping across the floor and the door slam closed behind the man would she crawl wearily back into her bed. More often than not, her mother would forget to check on the little girl until the next day.

Her mother, the town prostitute. Carrie shook her head. Somehow, the name "mother" didn't seem to fit the woman she had lived with the first ten years of her life. The men called her Sharayah. Carrie had never heard anyone say her mother's given name—not even Sharayah herself.

Carrie felt nauseated as she recalled the painful days of childhood. Things had gone from bad to worse as she grew older. The image of her mother from her fiery copper hair to her petite, well-shaped form, it wasn't long before the young girl was forced to endure the attentions of the evil-minded men.

Mercifully, Sharayah had taken ill, and young Carrie was sent to live with a kindly elderly woman, Grandma Esther. It had taken months of love and patience on Grandma Esther's part before Carrie could sleep the night through without waking with screams of fear.

Carrie had not shed a tear when her mother had died. Even now, a burning hatred filled her soul as she thought of Sharayah, dead for fifteen years. Determined to be as unlike her mother as possible, Carrie had chosen a life of serving others; a life of healing, not destroying. She had held her head high, ignoring the unkind whispers that had followed her. Though gradually gaining the confidence of the community, Carrie had not gained their friendship. Her past was not forgotten.

As a nurse, she found that she could somehow face the townspeople on a one-to-one basis, more or less hiding behind her medical knowledge. But it still took all the courage she could muster to mingle with a crowd. She could feel accusing eyes burning into her back; could hear the whispers floating around her. . .

She unconsciously pulled at her hair, drawing it back into an even tighter bun. "No, Sister Louisa," she said finally. "God doesn't love me."

four

Word spread quickly that Carrie was ill, and Zach suddenly had his hands full. He had never realized how many minor emergencies Carrie attended to throughout the week, both in town and out. After a few days of running himself ragged, however, Zach began to get the feeling that he was being tested by the townspeople. He was amused that they wanted him to prove himself. Confident he could win their favor, Zach knew he would have to beat them at their own game to do it.

The next day, he was up bright and early, ready for the onslaught. Sure enough, he was soon summoned to two different homes, each on the opposite side of town. After answering superfluous questions at both places, his amusement had faded. Arriving back at the boardinghouse in time for lunch, Zach was irritated to find a message waiting for him. "Not Mrs. Parker again," he groaned out loud. He had already been to see Annabelle's mother twice this week, and he had come to the conclusion that she had to be the whiniest woman he had ever met. Sighing, he grabbed an oatmeal cookie to eat on the way.

❧

"Oh, Dr. Tanner. Mother is *soooo* sick. I just don't know what to do." Tears shimmered in Annabelle's large violet eyes as she met Zach at the door.

Zach was disgusted. Entering Mrs. Parker's room, he found the plump woman in her bed, moaning in pain. Zach took his time examining her, suddenly quite certain he had found the instigator of his trials. "I'm afraid I have bad news," he said finally.

She gasped.

"What did you eat for supper last night, Mrs. Parker?"

29

"Well, I don't see how that. . ."

"We had cabbage soup, Dr. Tanner," Annabelle put in helpfully.

"Ah! That confirms it! I'm sorry, Mrs. Parker, but you have a severe case of gastrointestinal decompression." Zach stated the more serious-sounding diagnosis for gas pains.

The woman's mouth dropped open. "Why, I. . . What does that mean, Doctor?"

"Don't eat so much cabbage."

Mrs. Parker's eyes flashed. "You are unspeakably rude, Dr. Tanner. Why, Carrie always gives me a special drink whenever I feel this way." Turning her back to the doctor, she continued muttering under her breath.

Zach got up to leave, a smile twitching around the edges of his mouth.

"You handled Mother remarkably well, Dr. Tanner," Annabelle whispered to Zach as she escorted him to the door.

Zach gazed down at her, clearly amused with the whole situation. "Thank you, Annabelle."

Mysteriously, the number of "emergencies" were drastically reduced following Zach's call on Mrs. Parker, and life settled into a comfortably busy routine.

Carrie had laughed until she cried when Zach told her about Mrs. Parker. Zach had never heard her laugh before, and now he stared at her as if seeing her for the first time. The merriment had driven the ever-present shadows from her sapphire eyes, and a dimple flashed in her right cheek.

Her laughter quieted abruptly as she noticed Zach's eyes on her face.

Quickly assuming his usual non-threatening look, Zach smiled at her. *What I wouldn't give to bring the laughter back.* "What in the world do you give someone for a bad case of gas, Carrie? Mrs. Parker said you usually give her a special drink."

Another giggle escaped. "Iced peppermint tea with soda in it."

Zach raised his eyebrows. "That's the special drink?"

Carrie nodded. "I think she thinks it's some kind of secret drink that I made up just for her." She shrugged, still smiling. "Whatever makes her happy."

Zach stared at her. "I think I could learn a lot from you, Carrie."

She shrugged again as if unsure of what he meant. "I doubt that, Dr. Tanner. But I am feeling better every day. I'm moving back to my house tomorrow."

"Are you saying that you'll be going back to work soon?"

She nodded. "I've been in bed too long."

Zach leaned toward her. "How about it then, Carrie? Can we work together?"

She gazed at him, an unreadable look in her eye. "I knew you would ask me that." She stared past him for a moment, then looked at him directly. "Why do you want me to work with you, Dr. Tanner?" It was if she had asked herself that same question many times and had only now gathered the courage to ask him.

He was surprised. Surely she knew by now that his intentions were honest. "For one thing, I think we would do a better job if we were united in our efforts."

She nodded, apparently agreeing with the logic of his idea.

"Also, I think you and I could learn from each other, like I said a minute ago."

"Go on."

"That's about it, I guess, except that. . ." He paused, then watched in bewilderment as she visibly withdrew. It was as if she were one of the turtles from Larson's Pond, retreating into her protective shell whenever he got too close.

"I won't do it," she said softly.

He stared at her. "Do what?"

Her face flushed, sudden confusion clouding her brow. Had she misunderstood?

Zach felt his own face redden as he realized what she was thinking. What kind of man did she think he was, for Pete's sake? "All I was going to say was that it would be nice having a friend to work with, instead of always being alone."

Still she stared at him, as if trying to read his motives.

"Carrie?"

She studied him for a moment longer. "I will work with you, Dr. Tanner."

He smiled at her warmly, sensing the effort it had taken for her to even promise as much as she had. "I'm glad, Carrie." He reached for her hand, then thought better of it. Rising to his feet, he shook his finger at her playfully. "Now you get a good night's rest, young lady, or I'll fix you a special drink."

Her laughter rang out, and the sound of it lightened his spirit as he left the room.

Whistling as he headed home, he couldn't seem to erase the picture of her laughing face from his memory. His breath caught as he recalled her blue eyes dancing merrily; that adorable dimple in her cheek. Up until now, Zach had looked upon the young nurse as sort of a lost lamb; someone who needed healing in her soul; a person that God had sent for him to minister to.

Suddenly realizing that she was a woman was somewhat of a shock. Gritting his teeth as he thought of the horrors she had lived through, Zach made a vow to himself. *Father, with Your help, I will protect Carrie's honor and purity at all times. For in Your sight, Carrie's heart is innocent of the evils inflicted on her.*

Realizing now the heavy weight of responsibility that he had taken on, he cried out to God for wisdom. *Father, I know that You have entrusted this woman into my care, at least for a time. Please help me to lead her to You. Strengthen my heart that I will remain pure in my thoughts toward her. Give me wisdom. . . .*

Zach fell asleep peacefully that night, images of a joyful, peaceful Carrie floating through his mind. She worked side-by-side with him; laughing, learning, loving. . . .

❧

"You'll have to hold his head steady so I can sew it up,

Carrie," Zach whispered as he threaded the needle.

Carrie nodded. "Hal, Dr. Tanner is going to have to sew this gash closed." She looked the young man in the eye. "It's going to hurt, but you need to try to hold as still as possible. I'll help you."

Hal Weaver nodded slightly, his eyes glazed with pain. Zach and Carrie had had to walk several miles to reach the Weavers' homestead, and their patient had already lost a lot of blood.

"Here we go, Hal." Zach began the painstaking work of stitching closed the gaping wound that had been left by a horse's hoof.

Carrie held Hal's head firmly, whispering words of encouragement to the frightened young man. She watched as he clenched his fingers in pain, and wished there were something she could do to ease his suffering. The infusion of poplar bark she had given him would help somewhat, but she was sure he could still feel every pull of the needle.

"There." Zach carefully snipped off the length of catgut. "Forty-two stitches. I wouldn't let a horse step on my face again if I were you, Hal."

The young man smiled weakly. "Will it be all right?"

Zach nodded. "Make sure you keep it clean and dry, and it should heal up fine. I'll check up on you in a day or so. Oh, and drink that concoction Miss Winthrop brewed up for you. It will help with the pain." Zach gathered up his instruments, rinsed them with carbolic acid, then carefully washed his hands.

Carrie did likewise, and was already halfway to the door when Zach's next words stopped her in her tracks.

"Carrie, would you join me in prayer?"

She turned to look at him. He was standing by Hal's bedside, obviously waiting for her. She joined him hesitantly, then stared openly as he placed a gentle hand on Hal's forehead.

"Father, please touch Hal. I thank You for giving Carrie and me the ability to help him, but we're just instruments in

Your hands. Please complete the healing. Thank You. In Jesus' name, Amen."

Turning to give last-minute instructions to Hal's young wife, Zach failed to see Carrie's bewilderment.

Why would a doctor ask God to heal a patient? What could God do that Zach hadn't already done? Carrie was mystified.

Zach whistled as they made their way back to town. If he noticed Carrie's silence, he didn't mention it. Stopping on her front porch, he gazed at her earnestly. "Thank you, Carrie. You were a tremendous help to me."

She was embarrassed. "I had the easy part. I could never have stitched that up as neatly as you did."

Zach flashed her a boyish grin, making her heart turn over. "Practice makes perfect."

❧

The crisp autumn days flew by in a blur. With Carrie by his side and word of his reputation spreading, Zach found himself busier than he could have imagined. Miners, ranchers, gold diggers from far and near became familiar with the gentle young Dr. Tanner. Often he was gone for weeks at a time, making the rounds of mining camps and ramshackle shantytowns. Carrie continued to hold the fort in town, thankful that she no longer had to make the long, arduous journeys through the rough terrain.

Zach always treated Carrie in the same courteous manner, and she gradually grew less and less wary of him. At first it was if she had been looking for an ulterior motive on his part, but as the weeks turned into months, her reserve toward him began to melt.

❧

It was late one cold October night when he pounded on her door.

"Carrie! It's Zach! Hurry!"

"I'll be right there!" Yanking the door open two minutes later, she joined Zach on the porch. "What is it, Dr. Tanner?"

Zach caught his breath as he saw her framed in the light of

the open door. She was beautiful! Her blue eyes were wide, her hair hanging down her back in one long thick braid as stray tendrils curled about her sleep-flushed face.

With effort, he pulled his thoughts back to reality. "It's Buz Franklin, Carrie. I don't think he's going to make it through the night."

She gasped. "I'll get my bag."

Flying down the porch steps behind Zach, Carrie trotted to keep up with his long strides. "Is it pneumonia, Dr. Tanner?" They had been keeping a close eye on the elderly man for days, concerned that his chest cold would turn into pneumonia.

"I'm afraid so." Zach's voice was worried. "As soon as I got word from Marcy, I came for you. I haven't examined him yet, but I don't know what else it could be."

Carrie was silent. Zach knew she held a special place in her heart for the elderly couple. The Franklins always seemed to have had warm smiles and kind words for her—some of the few folks who hadn't shunned her socially.

&

Carrie was glad to enter the Franklins' cozy house after the long walk in the cold. Winter came early to the Rocky Mountains. She greeted Marcy with a hug as Zach went directly to the sick man's room. "How are you, Marcy?" she whispered.

The older woman's faded eyes filled with tears. "It's going to be all right, honey." She dabbed at her eyes with her apron. "The Lord promised me it's going to be all right."

Carrie smiled at her weakly. "I'm glad, Marcy." She patted the elderly woman's hand. "I need to go help Dr. Tanner now. You'll be all right?"

Marcy nodded, and Carrie went to join Zach. What could Marcy have meant? How could she know that God promised her something? Carrie had no time to ponder the meaning of Marcy's words as she concentrated on following Zach's instructions. Her heart ached to see her old friend Mr. Franklin suffering so, but her poise made it possible for her to put those feelings aside as she worked to save his life. She spoke to him in soothing tones as she applied the steaming compresses to his chest, hardly noticing as the hours flew by.

Suddenly she felt Zach's hand on her arm. His touch sent a jolt of electricity through her, and she whirled to face him. He stared down at her silently for a moment, an unreadable expression in his eyes. Finally he spoke, saying only, "It's going to be a long night, Carrie." He motioned to a comfortable-looking chair. "I want you to get some rest."

"But. . ."

"Carrie."

The look in his eye brooked no argument, so she obediently settled in the chair. Her arm still tingled where Zach's hand had been. She followed him with her eyes, watching as he tenderly cared for the dying man. What kind of man was Zach Tanner? She shook her head. He just didn't fit with what she thought men were like. Or what a doctor should be like, for that matter. Who ever heard of a doctor carrying a Bible in his medical bag?

Against her best intentions, Carrie's eyelids drooped, then closed. Sometime later, she awoke to the sound of Zach's low voice. Stretching stiffly, she felt the scratchy warmth of a wool blanket draped over her shoulders. Had Zach cared enough to cover her? She was about to stand up when she realized that he was praying. Leaning her head back and closing her eyes, she tried not to listen; but his quiet words flowed over her, seeping into her soul.

". . .and Father, I thank You that Buz and Marcy have had a full life of serving You. I thank You that they are Your children. Father, if it's time for Buz to come home to You, I pray that You would give Marcy strength. In the meantime, I pray that You would help Carrie and me to do our best. . . ."

Carrie's eyes flew open. Why would God help her do anything? He probably didn't even know who she was. And why did Dr. Tanner call God his Father? She frowned. *I don't even know who my father is.* She watched Zach as he rose to his feet, almost wanting to ask him more about God.

He motioned to her when he noticed she was awake. She stood next to him at Buz's bedside, marveling at the look of peace on the elderly man's face. *He must be doing much better,* she thought, relieved.

"It's time to call Marcy, Carrie."

She jumped at the seriousness in Zach's voice. "What do you mean, Dr. Tanner? His breathing is much clearer, and—"

"No, Carrie." Zach rubbed the back of his neck wearily. "His lungs just can't bear much more. He'll be gone by morning."

&

Two days later, Carrie stood at Marcy's side as Pastor Dan conducted the funeral. She didn't hear one word of his sermon; instead hearing Marcy's words ringing over and over in her mind. *It's going to be all right. . . The Lord promised me it's going to be all right. . .* Carrie frowned. *Buz dying was all right?* She glanced at Marcy. *True, she has a look of peace in her eyes, but—*

"Carrie!" Zach's whisper broke into her troubled thoughts. Stepping forward, she placed the tiny bouquet of wildflowers on the plain casket. They looked scraggly and small, but they were the only ones she had been able to find that hadn't already succumbed to the frosty nights. Moving back to Marcy's side, Carrie was startled as the elderly woman grasped her hand, squeezing it tightly. "You see? It is all right, dear. My Buz is in a far better place than us down here."

Carrie stared at her, wondering at the look on the widow's face. Then out of nowhere, a yearning filled Carrie's heart; a yearning to know that same peace. . .

five

Carrie groaned when the pounding on her door began at six o'clock Saturday morning. She had hoped to sleep in this morning, but apparently that wasn't to be. "I'm coming!" she yelled.

What could possibly be going on this time? Surely Sheila wasn't ready to have that baby yet. Carrie fumbled with her hair, awkwardly pinning it up with one hand as she reached for the door with the other.

Zach stood on her porch, grinning from ear to ear. "Good morning!"

Carrie blinked in the bright sunlight. "What is it, Dr. Tanner?"

His smile dropped slightly at the tone in her voice. "I'm sorry, Carrie. Did I wake you?" Without waiting for her answer, he plunged ahead like an excited schoolboy. "I just had to show you! Come on!" He bounded down the steps.

Carrie followed at a more sedate pace. *What on earth. . .?* "Oh!" She gasped as she saw the beautiful team of horses hitched to a brand-new wagon.

Zach beamed at her. "Do you like them?"

Carrie ran her hand over the horses' silky black coats. "They're beautiful," she breathed. "Are they yours?"

He nodded. "I'm tired of walking all over these mountains. Anyway, I figured it was high time for the doctor and his nurse to travel in style." He laughed at her startled look. "Come take a ride with me, Carrie."

She backed away, her hand going to pat her hair in a nervous gesture. "Oh no; I really shouldn't. . . ." Casting a longing glance at the horses, she gave in. "Just a short ride."

He helped her into the wagon, and she pretended not to notice the sparks that snapped between them when he touched

38

her hand. Tucked snugly under a wool blanket, Carrie felt like a princess in her carriage. "What are their names?" she asked after a moment.

"I thought maybe you would help me name them."

"Really?"

He nodded solemnly, hiding a smile at her eagerness.

"Well then, they might not have names for a little while, because I have to get to know them first." A sudden thought struck her. "Where are you going to keep them?" Mrs. Granger's boardinghouse didn't have any stables, if she recalled correctly.

"I thought maybe you would help me out with that as well." His tone was offhanded, but there was a gleam in his eye that she didn't miss.

"Oh?"

He hesitated. "I know it's a lot to ask, but could I possibly build a small barn on your property? I would pay you for the land, of course, and I would care for them. You wouldn't be burdened with that."

Carrie turned to look at him, her face radiant. "I would love to have them, Dr. Tanner," she whispered. "You don't have to pay me anything."

"Are you sure?" He frowned slightly.

She nodded. To have these glorious creatures nearby would be a dream come true. She had always loved horses, animals of any kind, in fact; but she never thought that she would actually be able to. . . . "May I help you care for them?"

Zach smiled at her warmly. "I'd be glad for the help."

She settled back into the seat happily. Looking around for the first time, it dawned on her that they were headed away from town. "Where are we going?"

Zach sneaked a quick look at her, seemingly pleased with her curiosity. "Oh, just to a favorite spot of mine. I thought you might like to see it."

They rode along in silence for several miles, enjoying the frost-gilded beauty around them. Carrie stole more than one glance at Zach, admiring the way he skillfully guided the team. Funny how she had never noticed before the way his thick brown hair curled slightly over his collar. . .

"Well, here we are!" Zach's cheery voice broke into Carrie's reverie, and she glanced about questioningly.

"Let me help you down." Zach's gentle hands had her on the ground in an instant. "It's not very far. Come on."

Carrie followed as he pushed through the underbrush. All at once, she heard rushing water. She sucked in her breath as the magnificent waterfall came into view. It had been years since she'd been to this spot, but it was still just as magnificent. "It's beautiful, Dr. Tanner! How did a newcomer like you find this local secret?"

"My family and I used to come here every summer for picnics," he answered quietly.

Carrie was startled. "Did you live around here?"

"Yes, I thought you knew that, Carrie. My family and I lived in Bailey until I was eight years old."

"Oh." If the Tanners moved when Zach was eight, that would have made Carrie about two years old at the time. She glanced at Zach, noticing the faraway look in his eyes.

Suddenly shaking his head as if to clear his mind, he turned to smile at her. "Shall we go closer?"

She nodded, her eyes bright with excitement. Compared to tiny Crow Creek that ran next to town, this stream was a raging river, beautiful in its intensity. Following the path that Zach made as he forged ahead, Carrie half-slid, half-walked down the steep embankment.

Zach reached the ground first. Gratefully, Carrie clung to his outstretched hand as she slid the last few steps down to the bottom. She started to pull her hand free, but Zach's grip tightened slightly. She glanced up at him, but he was staring at the waterfall. The thunderous crashing of the water discouraged conversation, so she turned slowly, joining him as he enjoyed the view.

She felt as if she were in a dream. The sheer force of the

waterfall was overpowering, but the feeling of her hand in Zach's stunned her. She could feel his warmth, and it was as if that warmth spread from their joined hands, filling her whole being. She shivered involuntarily, and Zach glanced down at her.

"Are you cold?" He mouthed the words.

She shook her head, unaware that her heart was revealed in her eyes.

Zach drew her slowly into his arms. Resting his chin on the top of her head, he held her gently for a long moment, as if he were afraid she would break. Then tipping her face up with one large hand, he gazed deep into her shocked blue eyes.

She stared at him wonderingly, his gentle touch telling her more than a hundred words ever could. Her pulse was thundering louder than the waterfall, and she dropped her gaze, unable to think of a single thing to say. He took her hand then and led her back up the trail to the waiting team. Lifting her into the wagon, he tucked the blanket around her with careful attention. Clucking to the horses, he drove slowly back to town.

❧

The barn went up faster than Carrie could have imagined, and soon her four-footed friends were right at home. She spent hours with them, thoroughly enjoying getting to know them. Then true to her word, she thoughtfully considered their personalities before naming them. Pepper was the first to be named.

Zach had nodded his approval. "Pepper fits her." He patted the prancing mare on her nose. "No one could ever accuse you of having a dull personality, Pepper."

"What did you name our other gal, Carrie?"

She smiled up at him. "I think you'll laugh, but I named her Molasses."

Zach raised his eyebrows. "Because she's so sweet?"

"And slow!" Carrie said. She had learned from experience, Molasses would not be rushed, no matter what the occasion.

Zach chuckled. "Does that mean I have to ride Molasses today?"

She raised her eyebrows.

"I bought a couple of saddles. Do you know how to ride?"

Carrie shook her head, her adrenalin pumping at the prospect of actually riding a horse.

"Well, there's no time like the present to learn. First I'll show you how to put the saddle on. . . ."

&

The bright winter days sped by. Carrie felt as if she were becoming a new person. Neither she nor Zach had mentioned what had happened that day near the waterfall, but Carrie could sense that something was different. Sometimes their hands would touch as they labored together over a patient, and a thrill would run through Carrie's body. What was happening to her?

You're being silly, she scolded herself one evening. She had been sitting by the fireplace trying to read, but images of Zach kept floating through her mind. Finally putting the book down, she stared into the fire. Her life had changed so much since the day Zach Tanner had knocked on her door. She shook her head. Had she really come to trust him? It hardly seemed possible; little by little he had won her over by his constant kindness and understanding. Yet, was that all there was to it? She sighed. Of course that was all there was. Dr. Tanner was kind and courteous to everyone, wasn't he? Then why did her heart beat faster when she felt his eyes on her? What about the day at the waterfall? She had felt his heart pounding furiously as she rested her head on his chest for that brief, heavenly moment. Even now she could recall the warmth of his breath on her hair, the clean scent of his skin.

Could it be possible that. . . No, she couldn't finish the thought. It was too unbelievable to think that someone like Zach Tanner could love her, Carrie Winthrop. After all, deep inside she was still the same frightened Carrie that she was the day he met her. Though she had come to trust one man, she was still bound by her past. Still an outsider, still an unwanted child, still a woman of shame.

She had managed to push the fear away lately in her new-found relationship with Zach, but it still lurked there, ready to overtake her at a moment's notice. No, she decided, it wasn't possible that Zach loved her. She wasn't worthy of anyone's love.

six

Carrie sat in the barn, patiently combing the burrs out of Pepper's tail. "I'm not going to ride you through Jorgensens' field anymore, that's for sure," she told the horse. A few minutes later she stood, stretching her aching muscles. Squinting as she made her way to the small tack room, she realized that dusk had fallen while she worked. These winter days were so short.

"Should've brought a lantern," she muttered. Groping around in the dark, windowless room, she finally succeeded in hanging the brush on its hook. She stepped out of the tack room into the dim light of the barn, then froze as she saw two shadowy figures standing in the doorway. She held her breath, hoping she wouldn't be seen.

Horrified, she watched as the men untied the horses and led them toward the door.

"No!" Without thinking, she ran toward the horses. The men whirled, and Carrie's heart stopped as she recognized Clarence Yeakley.

"Well, what do we have here?" The look on his face changed quickly from surprise to evil cunning. He strolled toward Carrie, chuckling as she shrank from his presence.

"Come on, Yeakley. Leave the girl alone." The other man shuffled his feet nervously. "I'm getting out of here."

Yeakley ignored his partner, his eyes fastened on Carrie.

She looked around in desperation. Could she make it to the door? Maybe if she diverted his attention somehow. . .

Yeakley followed her eyes, then shook his head. "Don't even try it, little Miss Goody-goody. I got a gun."

Carrie could see red spots swimming in front of her eyes. *I can't give up,* she thought frantically. *I've got to fight him.*

44

Willing her knees to stop shaking, she inched her way behind Pepper. Yeakley followed, causing the high-strung horse to prance nervously. Pepper's sudden snort startled Yeakley, and Carrie dove between the horse's legs to freedom.

She tore out of the barn, only to have Yeakley bring her down with a flying tackle. Jerking her to her feet, he pushed her up against the side of the barn.

"Not so fast, Sharayah." He leered at her. "Ya think yer too good for me, don't ya? Just because yer pa was. . ."

She wrenched herself out of his grasp for a second, but he was too fast. Pinning both of her wrists to the barn wall with one strong hand, he dropped his gun carelessly. "Don't move now," he commanded, his free hand fumbling with her hairpins. Her coppery hair spilled over her shoulders.

Tears began streaming down Carrie's face. *This couldn't be happening. . . .*

"Let her go, Yeakley." The low voice startled them both. Carrie sank to her knees as Yeakley whirled to face his challenger. His face blanched as it met the barrel of Zach's rifle.

"Don't move one muscle or you're dead."

Zach kicked Yeakley's gun away, then spoke to Carrie without taking his eyes off his captive. "Carrie, get me some rope from the barn."

She rose shakily, her heart still pounding like a bass drum. She held the rope out to Zach. He took it with one hand, keeping the rifle trained on Yeakley's temple. "Come here and hold this while I tie him up."

Carrie obeyed by sheer force of will, amazed at how steady her hands were.

"There." Zach finished tying Yeakley's hands, then squatted down to tie his feet. Laying the cursing man facedown on the frozen ground, Zach turned to Carrie. Taking the rifle from her, he leaned it against the barn, then gathered her in his arms.

"Zach!" Carrie collapsed against him, clinging to him as if for dear life. He held her tightly, stroking her hair as she sobbed.

"It's all right now, angel," he murmured soothingly. "You're safe now." Zach lifted his eyes heavenward, and she heard him whisper what sounded like a prayer.

Carrie pulled away from him just enough to peer into his eyes. "How did you know to come?"

He brushed away a tear that still clung to her cheek. "I think God sent me, Carrie," he said after a long moment. "You know I don't usually come to check on the horses this time of the evening, but I kept feeling that I had to come."

Carrie stared at him curiously. "I'm glad you did. Thank you."

Turning away slightly, he asked, "Are you afraid to stay alone for a little bit while I take this troublemaker in to the sheriff?"

"I'll be all right," she whispered, hating to admit to him how afraid she really was.

"I'll hurry, Carrie. I'll be back soon, I promise."

After seeing her to the front porch, Zach loaded his unwilling captive onto Pepper's back. "You're lucky I'm a God-fearing man, Yeakley," he growled. "I'm sure the law will be kinder to you than I would have been."

The man cursed again, and Zach stuffed a glove in his prisoner's mouth. "I'll not put up with that all the way to town!"

As Zach clucked to Pepper, Carrie sank down on the porch, still trembling.

౸

Zach dumped his prisoner unceremoniously in front of the jail. Banging on the door, he stood guard over the large man until the sheriff appeared. The lawman raised his eyebrows as Zach explained what had taken place.

The sheriff yanked Yeakley to his feet, chuckling as he saw the glove in the man's mouth. "I guess the good doctor had enough of your lip for one night, eh, Yeakley?"

Yeakley glared at Zach as he was led away, and Zach had the sinking feeling that he had made a lifelong enemy. Mounting Pepper, he rode back to Carrie's house deep in thought. He shook his head. What a terrifying experience for her to go through. It had all happened so fast that it was hard to recall the details.

When the terrible urgency to get to Carrie's house had come upon him, Zach had impulsively grabbed his rifle on the way out the door. He approached the barn in silence, the hair on the back of his neck prickling as he came upon the ugly scene. Hearing Carrie's sobs mingling with Yeakley's menacing tones, Zach sent up a quick plea for help, then made his move. His heart beat faster even now as he recalled the moment Yeakley had whirled to meet him. Zach had been sure he was going to have a gunfight with the larger man, and was surprised when he realized Yeakley's hands were empty.

He had to admit that he was as relieved as Carrie when he finally held her in his arms. His grim look softened as he remembered the feel of her hair brushing against his face; the way she had clung to him. An overwhelming urge to protect her forever grew within his breast, and Zach knew at that moment that he loved her. Nudging Pepper into a gallop, Zach hurried back to the woman who had unknowingly claimed his heart.

He found her sound asleep in front of the fireplace. Her long hair still tumbled over her shoulders; her face was pale and tear-streaked. She looked like a forlorn child. Zach scooped her up tenderly in his arms and carried her to her bedroom. Laying her on the bed, he covered her gently, then placed a soft kiss on her brow. "Sleep well, angel."

❧

Carrie awoke the next morning with a throbbing headache. *What a horrible dream—or was it?* She groaned as she fell back against the pillow, realizing that she was still wearing her dress. She closed her eyes as if to block out the ugly incident, thankful that Zach had come when he did. She shivered to think of what might have happened, feeling the familiar black fear creeping toward her. . . . She shook her head. It wouldn't do to think about those things. She tried to force her thoughts back to Zach, to stem the rising tide of fear that threatened to grip her. But she couldn't escape. Not even Zach's strong arms or loving words could save her. She moaned, the fear engulfing her like a flood, until dawn's light peeked timidly through the window to give temporary respite to the darkness of her soul.

&

She woke again with a start, drenched with sweat. Every night it was the same, and she began to dread going to sleep. The nightmares that she had not experienced in months came back with a vengeance, and she would awaken night after night, screaming in terror. Always Clarence Yeakley would be chasing her, sometimes accompanied by other faceless men. She could hear Yeakley's voice over and over. "Ya think yer too good, don't ya? Just because yer pa. . ." Who was her pa? *Are you out there, Papa?* Sometimes Yeakley's leering face would turn into the face of her father. She didn't know him, yet he would chase her, on and on. . . .

&

Zach had expected Carrie to relapse into her old pattern of fear and wariness after the ugly incident, but it didn't happen. At first he was pleased, wondering at her seemingly nonchalant attitude. True, Clarence Yeakley was in jail and wouldn't be able to bother her for a long time, but. . .

He soon suspected that the incident had frightened her much more than she let on. He began to watch her carefully, feeling that his suspicions were proven correct when she began looking hollow-eyed and haggard. Soon she began to withdraw, even from him. He prayed for her daily, his heart breaking at the fear and pain she was experiencing. He longed to hold her, but restrained himself, knowing she needed time to heal. Knowing also that only the Great Physician could heal a broken heart, he treated her with great tenderness day by day, hoping to see a change for the better.

Noticing one day how thin she had become, Zach was seized with an inspiration. Hitching up the team, he called to

Carrie. "I'll be back in an hour, Carrie. Put some warm clothes on." Without waiting for her reply, he drove out of the yard.

True to his word, he returned shortly. He was pleased to find Carrie waiting for him with her hat and gloves. He swung her up in the seat, refraining from commenting on her stick-thin figure.

She was silent as he clucked to the horses.

"Don't you want to know where we're going?" He glanced at her.

She shrugged. "Just so it's not to town," she said tiredly. He had noticed that she had been avoiding the townspeople as much as possible lately, probably feeling that everyone would blame her for the incident with Yeakley.

Zach whistled as he drove, praying silently. He thought he detected a small spark of interest in her eye as they neared the waterfall, and was glad. Lifting her down from the wagon, he let his hands linger lightly on her waist until she looked up. He gazed deep into her shuttered eyes for a long moment, willing her to understand his love for her. "You can trust me, Carrie," he whispered finally. "Do you know that?"

He watched as her eyes filled with tears. "I want to, Zach." Her voice was barely audible.

He pulled her to him then, letting her feel his strength. "Let me share your burden, sweet Carrie," he murmured. "You don't need to bear it alone."

She nodded her head against his chest, then pushed away from him to stare at the waterfall.

Zach began busily digging around in the back of the wagon. He pulled a huge basket out and tucked a blanket under his arm. He walked past Carrie, spread the blanket on the frozen ground, and opened the basket. As he pulled out container after container of food, the sound of Carrie's low chuckle startled him. It had been too long since he heard her laugh. He glanced up at her.

"You must be very hungry, Dr. Tanner," she said, eyeing the feast.

Zach grinned, relieved at her lightened mood. "I was hoping there would be some left for me after you finished," he teased.

She raised her eyebrows. "I think there's enough food there to last three days."

"Well, I know one way to find out," Zach said, grabbing a huge ham sandwich. He said a quick blessing, then bit into the sandwich with relish.

He watched as Carrie took a much smaller bite. "I coaxed Mrs. Granger into making all this for me," he confessed, waving his hand at the food. "I'll probably have to hang her laundry out for a month to repay her."

Carrie gave a small smile at the doleful look on Zach's face. "At least she's a good cook."

Zach leaned back against a tree, patting his full stomach. "That chocolate cake was worth a year of laundry."

She smiled at him, and his heart turned over. Maybe it was the right time to plant a little seed.

seven

"Did you ever have a patient that refused to do what you told him to do, even though it would make him well?"

Zach's sudden question jolted Carrie from her reverie. She stared at him thoughtfully for a moment, then smiled as she thought of little Jimmy Baker refusing to take his castor oil. "Once in a while, I guess. Why do you ask?"

Zach ignored her question, settling himself more comfortably against the tree. "I once knew a man who was deathly ill," he began, lacing his fingers behind his head. "He knew I was a doctor and that I could probably give him something that would cure him."

Carrie nodded, wondering at the wistful look in his eye.

"I went to his house many times, but he wouldn't let me touch him." Zach shook his head. "Said he didn't want me wasting my time on him—that he was too sick and too old."

"I've never heard of such a thing!" Carrie was appalled. "Did he die?"

Zach nodded. "I'm afraid so." He studied the ground for a moment, then lifted his eyes to meet her gaze. "I'm afraid you're like that man, Carrie."

His words struck her as if he had punched her in the stomach. "What do you mean?" she whispered. "I'm not sick."

"No, Carrie. You're not physically sick." Zach's voice was gentle. "But you have some wounds in your soul that need to be taken care of."

Carrie dropped her gaze. *Was it still that obvious?*

"Carrie." His earnest tone made her look up. "I wish I had some medicine that would instantly take away your pain, but I don't. I'm only a doctor." Zach touched her cheek gently. "But I know One who *can* heal those wounds."

51

She stared at him, her heart pounding strangely at the thought of being free from fear and shame. Surely Zach was referring to God, but how. . .?

"Carrie, God is waiting for you to let Him love you."

She shook her head, the sorrow returning full force after the brief leap at hope. "God doesn't love me, Zach."

"Ah, but you're wrong, Carrie. Listen to this." Zach grabbed his ever-present Bible, turning the pages confidently until he found the verse he was looking for. "John 3:16 says, 'For God so loved the world, that he gave his only begotten Son, that whosoever believeth in him should not perish, but have everlasting life.' " Zach put the Bible down. "That means all of us, Carrie. God sent His Son to everyone."

"But. . ." Her confusion was evident on her face. "How could God love me? I don't even know who my father is. I'm nothing. I—"

"Carrie." The compassion in Zach's eyes halted her flow of words. "God is the Great Physician. Don't be like the man who refused to let me help him." He looked her directly in the eye. "*None* of us is worthy of God's love, Carrie. We're all sinners."

"But you don't know. . ." Her face flamed as scenes from her childhood flashed through her mind.

"It doesn't matter, Carrie." Zach's voice was firm with assurance. "Nothing you could ever do, or have done to you, could make God stop loving you."

She frowned, trying to absorb the meaning of his words. It sounded wonderful, but somehow she just could not accept that God loved her. "I'll think about what you've said, Zach," she said finally. It was the best she could do.

Zach smiled at her. "Good." He stood up and stretched. "How about a walk down to the bottom of the waterfall?"

"I'd. . .like that."

They scrambled down the steep embankment together like carefree children. Once on the ground, they paused as one to gaze at the crashing water. The majestic beauty touched

Carrie deeply. *Could a God who had created something as awesome as this have a place in His heart for me?* It was an amazing idea.

She looked up at Zach, her heart suddenly overflowing with happiness. It was wonderful to be in this place, with the man she loved. . . . The man she loved? She watched in fascination as Zach's eyes darkened with emotion. He pulled her to him slowly, tentatively. She welcomed his embrace, joy rushing through her at his touch. He gently cupped her chin in his hand, watching her face questioningly as he lowered his lips to hers. The kiss was achingly tender, filled with unspoken promises. Zach pulled away first, reaching out a trembling hand to smooth her hair back.

Carrie gazed up at him, unable to speak. Why had he kissed her? Could it be that he loved her? He had promised not to hurt her. . . . She touched her lips. "I'm not afraid of you." Her words were a mere whisper floating on the frosty air, as if her wondering thought had escaped out of her mouth of its own accord.

Zach hugged her to him happily. "I'm glad." Suddenly, a gleam of fun danced into his eyes. "Let's go exploring."

Grasping Carrie's hand, he coaxed her nearer the water's edge. "If you look carefully, you might see the fish."

Carrie bent down, watching intently. A flash of silver caught her eye, and she pointed triumphantly. "There!"

Zach looked to where she was pointing. "Yep, that's a trout. A nice fat one, too. I should have brought my fishing pole."

Carrie reached into the water for a glittering stone. "Oh!" The coldness of the water made her jerk her hand back quickly.

Zach laughed. "That's pure melted snow, remember? Comes from up there." He gestured toward the high mountain peaks that surrounded them. "I'll have to bring you back here in the spring. If you think the waterfall is spectacular now, you should see it when the spring melt is on."

Carrie smiled up at him, warmed by the feeling of trust and

friendship between them. She wouldn't dare call it anything else. Not on purpose, at least.

෨

Christmas was quickly approaching, and Carrie looked forward to it with all the eager anticipation of a child. She had never celebrated Christmas until she went to live with Grandma Esther, but even then it had been a quiet, solemn celebration. But this year! Her eyes glowed with excitement. Zach had asked her to accompany him to the annual Christmas social.

Though she had lived in this town all her life, she had never attended the gala event. But with Zach by her side, she could do it. She could face all those pairs of eyes with her head held high. She waltzed through the house in a dream, dust cloth in hand. Catching a glimpse of herself in the mirror, she frowned at her reflection. Somehow, the drab dresses she was accustomed to wearing didn't match the new sparkle in her eyes. Putting the dust cloth down thoughtfully, she loosened the tight knot of hair at the back of her head.

The nightmares had become less and less frequent lately, replaced by dreams of Zach. Instead of visions of faceless pursuing men, her night hours were filled with the never-ending refrain of Zach's words. ". . .God loves you, Carrie. . .loves you. . .loves you. . .wants to heal you. . . ."

True to her word, Carrie had thought long and hard about what Zach had said that day at the waterfall. The result of meditating on those words of hope stared back at her now from the mirror. The tight lines of suspicion and wariness had all but disappeared from around her mouth and her eyes had taken on a slight sparkle, an anticipation of life. Though she did not yet know it herself, she had begun the walk down the path to freedom.

෨

Zach had noted a subtle change in Carrie, and he rejoiced. The night of the Christmas social, he arrived on her doorstep an hour early. A rush of warm air greeted him as Carrie opened the door, and Zach caught his breath when he saw her. She wore a dress that matched exactly the color of her dancing eyes, and though her hair was still pulled back too severely and the dress appeared large on her still too-thin figure, something about her was different. Perhaps it was because he had never seen her in any other color than gray or brown—or was it the glow in her gorgeous eyes?

He stopped contemplating and pulled her into his arms. "You look very beautiful tonight, Nurse Carrie," he murmured in her ear. The warm scent of her skin made him dizzy, and he gently pushed her away before he completely lost his senses.

She smiled up at him, seeming not to notice the fire she had ignited within him. "Thank you, Doctor."

He returned her smile, willing his heart to stop racing. "Come on. I have something in the barn I want you to see." Maybe some fresh air would clear his mind.

"What?" Carrie blinked at the abrupt change of direction.

"Put your coat on. Come on!"

She obeyed, following him outside. Stepping into the warmth of the barn, he saw her look for something out of the ordinary. She looked at Zach questioningly.

He grinned at her. "Wait here."

He ducked into Molasses' stall, and scuffled briefly with the tiny ball of fur before he backed slowly out of the stall. Turning to her, he held out a small brown puppy.

"Oh, Zach!" Carrie reached out for the trembling animal, cuddling the puppy to her. Noticing the note attached to the red bow around his small neck, she read it aloud.

"Dearest Carrie, Here is a small someone for you to love. Merry Christmas! Yours, Zach." The puppy licked her chin as if to second the sentiment. "Thank you," she whispered, choking back her emotion. "I can't believe he's really mine."

Zach was immensely pleased with her reaction. "You're welcome," he said quietly, enjoying the glow of happiness on her face. "Now it won't be so lonely at your house."

❧

He was touched when Carrie gave him the navy gloves and muffler she had knit for him. "I guess my patients won't have to complain about my cold hands anymore, now." He chuckled.

"I'm glad you like them." She reached for her coat. "Shall we go to the church now?"

"In a minute." Zach hunted through his coat pocket. "I have one more gift for you." Pulling out a small, plainly wrapped box, he handed it to her solemnly.

"But you already gave me the puppy," she protested.

He shrugged. "I want you to have this, Carrie."

Tearing off the wrapping, she lifted the lid, gasping as she recognized the familiar brown leather cover. "Oh, Zach. It's your Bible! I can't take this."

"I want you to have it, sweetheart," he repeated, closing her fingers around the precious Book. "It's helped me through a lot of rough places."

Tears gathered in her eyes. "I'll treasure it always, Zach."

He gazed into her eyes. "Do more than treasure it, Carrie. Read it."

"I will, Zach. I will."

❧

The Christmas social was more than Carrie had imagined. With Zach by her side, it was easy to enter the brightly lit, bustling church building. Accustomed as she was to watching as others had fun, Zach had to coax her into joining in the fun and games. Soon she was swept up into the merriment, laughing more than she had ever laughed in her life. Carrie noted that Pastor Dan and Sister Louisa watched approvingly from across the room.

Zach at last walked her over to a table where Sister Louisa had just settled and excused himself, promising to bring back some refreshments.

Carrie dropped into a chair next to Sister Louisa. "Merry Christmas, Louisa," she said happily.

"And to you, too, dear." The older woman took in Carrie's

sparkling eyes and flushed cheeks. "How is it with you, child?"

Carrie smiled. "It's wonderful, Sister Louisa."

Louisa's eye held a knowing look. "*It's* wonderful or *he's* wonderful?" she teased.

Carrie's cheeks grew even redder. "Both," she admitted, glancing over to where Zach stood visiting with a group of men. "I never knew—"

"Attention, please!" Pastor Dan's voice broke into the women's conversation. "If everyone will carry their own chair over here, it's time for the children's play to begin."

Zach came over to help Carrie with her chair. Together they sat down to watch the beloved Christmas story acted out by the children of the town.

All the candles were extinguished except the one at the front, and an expectant hush fell over the crowd. Zach threaded his fingers through Carrie's as Pastor Dan began to read the ancient words from the Gospel of Luke. "And it came to pass in those days, that there went out a decree from Caesar Augustus, that all the world should be taxed. . . ."

Carrie sat transfixed as the story unfolded. It was as if she had never heard it before. Mary's pain became as Carrie's own when the townspeople turned against the young woman. Tears came to her eyes as Joseph decided to put away his young wife, then dried as the angel appeared to Joseph, telling him not to be afraid. Carrie held her breath as the young couple went from inn to inn seeking shelter in crowded Bethlehem. When finally the blessed Baby was born, she felt as if her heart would burst with joy. At last she understood. Jesus was God's own Son, born for the world—born for her. She wanted to run and kneel with the tiny child-shepherds, to worship the One sent for her, for Carrie Winthrop.

Zach felt her trembling, and squeezed her hand tightly. She knew he couldn't see her face in the dim light, but she didn't care if he saw her tears of joy flowing freely.

"It's true!" she whispered. "He really does love me. God loves me!"

eight

"Just a minute, little one." Carrie pushed the puppy away gently. She sighed as she closed Zach's Bible. It had seemed so real, so simple, that night at the Christmas play. But now. . .

Her hand brushed the Bible's leather cover and she smiled as she thought of the man who had given it to her. She had been plying Zach with questions ever since the play, trying to understand.

"How can I be sure that God loves me, Zach? I don't even know Him. Besides, I—"

"Ah, Carrie. Don't doubt your heart." Zach smiled at her. "Don't you remember what you realized the night of the Christmas play, that God had sent His Son for you?"

"Yes, but I don't feel anything now. I guess I understand now that Jesus came for everyone, but why would He want to love me?"

"That's your problem right there, Carrie. You don't think you are worthy of His love, do you." Zach's words were a statement, not a question.

She dropped her gaze, then looked up at Zach through pain-filled eyes. "I could never be worthy of anyone's love, Zach," she cried in despair. "You should know that."

He took a deep breath. "Carrie," he began gently, "it's true that we have all sinned. Every single person in the world has sinned and needs to ask God's forgiveness. When we ask God's forgiveness, we become worthy in His eyes, because of Jesus. Do you understand?"

"Not really," Carrie whispered.

Zach picked up the Bible. "Do you believe that this is God's Word, Carrie?"

She nodded.

"Does God lie?"

Blue eyes flew to meet his. "No, of course not. He's perfect, isn't He?"

Zach nodded. "Yes, He is. And He sent Jesus to us, to bear our sins for us on the cross. Do you know why He did that?" Zach grasped Carrie's hand. "Jesus took our sins on Himself, so we don't have to carry them anymore. When we ask God to forgive our sins, He remembers that Jesus already bore all those sins. Because of the blood that Jesus shed, we are seen as righteous and worthy in God's eyes."

Carrie frowned. "You make it sound so easy. But even if we can be made worthy in God's eyes, why would He *want* to love us?"

"We are His creation, Carrie. He is our Heavenly Father. To not love us would be like a mother who doesn't love her child."

Carrie could understand that. "My mother didn't love me," she admitted. "I just don't know, Zach. It's starting to make sense, but—"

"It's all right, Carrie. Ask God to show you the way, and He will."

ॐ

Ask God to show you the way. . . . The words had echoed in her mind for days. Could it be that easy? Unable to ignore the insistent nudging of a small nose against her leg, Carrie lifted the squirming puppy onto her lap.

"What am I going to name you?" she asked him absently, her mind still on her conversation with Zach. The small pup nestled into her arms, falling asleep almost instantly. Carrie smiled down at the small ball of fur. *It must be wonderful to feel so warm and secure,* she mused. Laying her head back, she imagined what it would be like to rest in Zach's arms; secure in his love. . . .

She stretched stiffly, her aching body telling her that she had been asleep in the chair for quite a while. Placing the puppy on his blanket by the fireplace, she made her way to the kitchen. Spying the huge plate of leftovers that Sister Louisa had insisted she bring home with her from the social, she fixed herself a generous helping. Shivering, she carried her plate back into the living room and threw another log on the fire. She settled comfortably in the rocker with her plate and the puppy.

Zach's Bible caught her eye once again. As she picked it up, it fell open to the first page. *Christmas 1878. "The grass withereth, the flower fadeth: but the word of our God shall stand for ever." Isaiah 40:8. To my loving husband, Thaddeus Green. Love, May* read the inscription written across the top of the page. Underneath it were the words written to Zach: *To our dear son Zach on his graduation: We know your father would have wanted you to have his Bible. We are so proud of you, son, and thankful that you have chosen to follow the words of this Book. Our love and prayers are with you always. Love, Mama and Papa.*

Carrie puzzled over these words until she had gathered the courage to ask Zach about them.

"My father passed away when I was just a youngster, Carrie," he had said quietly. "I can barely remember him."

"How did it happen, Zach?"

"I don't know much about it, except that he was shot in a hunting accident. I never wanted to ask my mother about it because I know that it still brought her pain whenever his name was mentioned."

The subject had been dropped then, but Carrie still wondered why Zach had seemed so vague about it. Shrugging, she turned back to the Bible. The third inscription was addressed to her. *Christmas 1910. Dearest Carrie, May the words of this Book be the key that unlocks the secrets of life. The answer to every question can be found within—just ask and look. Merry Christmas, Zach.*

❧

Carrie and Zach had their hands full as winter took its toll with croup and pneumonia. Night after night the young doctor and his nurse took turns sitting by the bedsides of crying children and suffering adults. The children were the hardest; Carrie's heart went out to the parents as they stood by helplessly. "If God loves everyone, why do these children have to suffer so?" Carrie finally blazed at Zach after another long, agonizing night.

He turned weary eyes on her face. "I don't know, Carrie, except that we don't live in a perfect world." He turned back to the small child who was struggling to catch her breath after a spasm of coughing. "All we can do is pray that they make it through."

Carrie shook her head. *I'm not going to pray to a God that lets His children suffer so,* she vowed to herself. She clamped her lips in a firm line and went about her tasks grimly. *If the children did pull through, it wouldn't be because of God. It would be because of my own hard work.* After little Ina Grey died of the croup, Carrie put Zach's Bible away. She didn't need a God that treated His children like that.

꙳

The winter gradually slipped into spring, and Carrie slipped back into her old ways. Zach noticed and seemed puzzled, but said nothing. One day he proposed a jaunt to the waterfall spot.

"I don't think so, Zach," she replied tiredly. Even her relationship with Zach seemed to have lost its luster. Everything was gray, and Carrie felt herself regressing into her old familiar pit of fear and bitterness. She plodded lethargically through the days and cried herself to sleep at night. Finally rousing herself one morning after another restless night, Carrie studied herself in the mirror. Dull blue eyes looked back at her, taking in the drab dress and unkempt hair.

"Something has got to change," she said aloud.

꙳

Zach objected strenuously when Carrie told him of her plan to leave Bailey. "Where will you go?"

She made an impatient gesture with her hand. "Just away, Zach. I don't know. Probably to Denver City. Maybe I'll go to school and become a real nurse."

Zach ignored her last sarcastic remark. "At least stay with my parents for a few days until you find a place to go," he had pleaded. "They live in Denver."

Carrie had refused, but Zach won her over with his argument that his mother needed a nurse anyway. "She really is getting to be too much for Papa to handle alone after her last stroke," Zach had said.

૪૦

Now as she stood nervously on the Tanners' front porch, Carrie wasn't so sure this was such a good idea. But before she could turn to leave, a large man opened the door.

"I thought I heard someone out here," he boomed, extending his hand. "Welcome, young lady. You must be Carrie."

"Yes, sir." Carrie was taken aback by the man's friendliness.

"Well, come on in and meet May. By the way, my name is Charles, not 'sir.' "

Carrie had to smile at the twinkle in his eye. This might not be so bad after all.

Following Charles into the bedroom, she was greeted by Zach's mother. Unable to speak, the frail woman motioned to Carrie to come closer to the bed, then enfolded the younger woman in a surprisingly firm embrace.

Carrie pulled away, embarrassed. "It's nice to meet you, Mrs. Tanner," she murmured.

The elderly woman shook her head vigorously, giving her husband a meaningful glance.

Charles chuckled. "She wants you to call her May, Carrie. I told you!"

"All right, May." Carrie smiled, her heart turning over when May smiled back. *That smile looked just like Zach's.* "Do you know how much your son looks like you?"

May beamed. "He's a good boy," she scribbled on her tablet.

"Yes, he is, May," Carrie agreed, swallowing against the sudden ache in her throat.

&

Carrie's days at the Tanners' soon fell into a comfortable routine. In the morning, Charles would help her lift May from the bed. Carrie would bathe her, then freshen the bed while May sat in her chair by a sunny window. After May was tucked back in bed, it was time to read. The Tanners had a large collection of books, and Carrie soon found that she enjoyed reading as much as May enjoyed listening.

Though May could no longer speak, she could laugh, and the two women spent many happy hours together. Soon Carrie took to sharing humorous stories of life in Bailey. May listened and watched, observing the younger woman's face carefully.

One day May had a different request. Instead of the novel they had been reading, she pointed to her Bible. Watching as Carrie reluctantly pulled it from the shelf, May's eyes took on a knowing gleam. Grasping her pencil, she scribbled on her pad, then handed it to Carrie.

"Read Second Corinthians five, please," Carrie read. Gingerly flipping through the pages, Carrie found the passage without too much trouble. True to her resolve, Carrie had not opened Zach's Bible once since she had put it away that night so long ago. Now as she began to read, she couldn't keep her voice from trembling.

May sat with her eyes closed, seemingly oblivious to Carrie's turmoil. Carrie faltered, then began to read swiftly. However, the healing words made their mark in her hungry heart, and by the time she reached verse 17, she was reading slowly, thoughtfully. " 'Therefore if any man be Christ, he is a new creature: old things are passed away; behold, all things are become new.' "

All things are become new? How could that be? Carrie glanced at May. The older woman appeared to be sleeping, so Carrie rose and placed the Bible back on the shelf thoughtfully. *How could all the old things pass away? Surely God didn't forget about things, did He?*

Carrie tried to sleep, but images of Zach filled her mind. His arms tight around her. . .his gentle voice as he comforted a sick child. . .his tender words as she left for Denver. . . *"I'll miss you very much, Carrie. Come back to me soon."*

I can't come back yet, Zach, her heart cried. *I can't come back until I can come back as a whole person. . .until the old things have passed away. . . .*

nine

Zach glanced over his shoulder for the third time. Seeing nothing, he turned back around, but the feeling of unseen eyes on his back caused his neck to prickle. Urging Pepper into a fast trot, he smiled at his own foolishness. Ever since Clarence Yeakley had broken out of jail two weeks ago, Zach had been on his guard.

He's probably miles from here by now, he chided himself. Still, he had to admit that for the first time since Carrie had left, he was glad she was gone. At least he didn't worry about Yeakley bothering her. The thought gave him great satisfaction. As far as he knew, she was still with his parents in Denver, and though he longed for her, he was thankful to have at least a small link with her. *If anyone can help Carrie understand the way to God, it's Mama and Papa,* he thought affectionately.

Lost in thought, Zach ignored the subtle rustling of the bushes just ahead of him.

"Zach! Dr. Tanner!"

Zach started as Pastor Dan came flying down the road toward him.

"Thank God I found you, son! Laura Polls has been in labor all night and she's in a bad way. Molly has been tending her, but she thinks the baby's turned wrong, and. . ."

❧

Zach sighed in frustration. What he wouldn't give right now for Carrie's help. "All right, Laura." He spoke firmly to the exhausted young woman. "I know you're tired, but it's almost over. I need you to get on your hands and knees."

Laura glanced at him in disbelief, sweat pouring from her face.

"You can do it, Laura. It might help the baby turn. Get up!"

The sternness of Zach's voice shocked her as he hoped it would, and she glared at him as she struggled to obey. The women on either side helped her up. Panting, she gasped suddenly. "He turned! I felt it!"

"Thank God!" Zach closed his eyes for a brief second. "Now, we're going to have to work fast. Molly, be ready to assist me. Sarah, have my instruments laid out, please."

Ten minutes later, a lusty cry sounded as Jacob Henry Polls entered the world. Laura collapsed in exhaustion, and Zach and his makeshift nurses nearly danced in relief.

Moments later, Zach handed Laura her baby. "The Lord is good, Laura," he whispered. She smiled up at him, then turned wondering eyes on the little one in her arms.

Zach smiled at the tender scene, turning away abruptly as unexpected tears sprang to his eyes. Suddenly it wasn't Laura he saw lying there, but Carrie, holding his baby—their baby. Zach brushed the moisture from his eyes. *Let it be, please, Lord,* he prayed fervently. *One day, let it be. . . .*

இ

It was always good to get a letter from home. Zach opened it eagerly, flopping down on the bed as he began to read. Mama couldn't speak anymore, but she still had enough control to write. Though her once-beautiful penmanship was now almost an illegible scrawl, it meant all the world to her son just to know she was thinking of him. His heart beat faster as he came to the last lines of the letter.

> *Carrie and I have become quite close. She is so hungry for love and acceptance, as I'm sure you know. She reminds me of a small wounded sparrow, but I know that God is working in her heart. I can see small changes every day. Keep on praying for her, son. Don't give up.*
>
> *I love you,*
> *Mama*

P.S. She loves you, you know.

Zach stared at the last words. As much as he hoped they were true, he knew that there was no real love without trust. *Only You can give us true love for each other, Father. Please continue to heal Carrie and bring her back to me, Lord. . .*

His prayers were interrupted by a sharp rap on the door. "It's six o'clock, Dr. Tanner," Mrs. Granger hollered.

Zach groaned. He had forgotten that he was to go to the Parkers' house for supper. He had some business matters to discuss with Mr. Parker, and the older man had insisted that Zach come to the house.

"I'd just as soon meet at your office, Mr. Parker," Zach had protested.

"Nonsense! The girls would love to have you."

"That's what I was afraid of," Zach murmured. "I'll be there at six-thirty," he had finally promised, not wanting to seem rude.

Now as he straightened his jacket and combed his hair, Zach wasn't sure why he had consented. *An evening with Annabelle and her mother was enough to drive anyone to an early grave,* he mused. Perhaps that was why Mr. Parker usually worked so late at the bank.

❧

"It was so nice of you to come, Dr. Tanner."

Zach grimaced as Annabelle's gushing began.

"Mother fixed a special supper just for you."

Probably cabbage rolls, Zach thought irritably as Annabelle prattled on. Soon Mr. Parker made his appearance, rescuing Zach from his daughter. "The good doctor and I have some business to attend to, Belle. Run along now and help your mother."

Zach heaved a sigh of relief as Mr. Parker ushered him into the library. Zach had the grace to blush as the older man glanced at him in amusement. "My sentiments exactly, son."

Zach was in a decidedly cheerier mood after talking with Mr. Parker. The business had been conducted more smoothly than Zach had anticipated, and he was able to tolerate the hour at the dinner table with a fair amount of good humor.

"Dinner was delicious, Mrs. Parker," he said as they rose from the table.

"Too bad you can't enjoy good home cooking more often, eh, Doctor?" Mr. Parker chuckled. "A good wife would get you fixed up in no time at all."

Zach sent a withering glance in Mr. Parker's direction as Annabelle eagerly grasped his arm. "Daddy's right, you know," she whispered as they walked to the door.

Zach ignored the comment. "Thank you for the nice evening, Annabelle," he said politely.

❧

He whistled lightly as he walked the few blocks back to Mrs. Granger's. The night was clear and he admired the starry sky as he walked. He wished Carrie were walking beside him, her hand enfolded in his—

He whirled at the small sound, his mouth going dry as Clarence Yeakley stepped from behind a tree.

"Sounds like yer havin' a purty happy evening, Doc," he snarled.

"What do you want, Yeakley?"

"I think you know what I want, Tanner," Yeakley replied menacingly, inching his way toward Zach. "You think yer pretty slick, doncha? Playing around with the banker's daughter while yer purty little nurse tramp is gone."

Zach felt the blood rush to his face, his anger driving away all traces of fear. "Don't ever speak of Carrie in that way again, Yeakley." His voice was a low growl. "I may be a God-fearing man, but I'll—"

He wasn't prepared for the stunning blow that caught him under the chin. The next thing he knew, Yeakley sat on top of him. The big man stared down at Zach. "I was jest goin' to shoot ya," he reflected, "but I think it'll be more fun to watch ya suffer."

Yanking Zach to his feet, Yeakley sent him crashing to the ground again with a vicious kick. Zach groaned as he struggled to protect himself against his opponent's fierce blows. His last thoughts were of Carrie, and then the blackness came.

ten

Carrie leaned back against the headboard. It was funny how she had never even thought to look for another place to go after coming here six weeks ago. The Tanners just made her feel so loved, like she was part of their family. It seemed like some sort of wonderful dream.

I wonder what they would think if they knew who I really am, she thought idly. Somehow, she couldn't envision May and Charles Tanner turning anyone away, no matter who they were. The thought made her feel warm inside. *Zach says that that's how God is,* she remembered suddenly.

Zach—an image of him standing by the waterfall popped into her mind, and a pang shot through her. She sighed. Would she ever be able to give and receive love freely?

❧

Charles knocked on her door early one morning. "Rise and shine, sleepyhead!" he called through the door.

Carrie appeared in the kitchen moments later to find him surrounded by mounds of toys. "What on earth?"

Charles grinned at her. "May said today is the day, so today it is."

Carrie stared at him blankly.

"Go see May. She'll explain."

Zach's mother was waiting for Carrie with a big smile and more toys.

"What is this all about, May?" Carrie gestured toward the kitchen where Charles was singing at the top of his lungs.

May handed her tablet to Carrie. "Today is Blessing Day," Carrie read. "What?"

Charles came into the room then. "May collects these toys throughout the year, Carrie." He gestured to the dolls and

69

trucks that cluttered the floor. "When the right day comes, we wrap them up and take them to the orphanage."

"Oh. But how do you know what day is the right day?"

May thumped her chest.

Charles chuckled. "She says she just knows it in her heart."

"Oh." Carrie was still slightly bewildered, but it sounded like a nice thing to do. After getting May ready for the day, she helped Charles finish wrapping the toys in gaily decorated paper.

"May and I always went together to deliver the toys," he said wistfully, staring at a tiny doll. "I guess this year you and I will have to make sure we tell her everything that happens."

❧

"This is the same orphanage that May grew up in, you know," Charles remarked as they arrived at the huge gray building.

Carrie turned questioning eyes on him. "I didn't know May grew up in an orphanage!"

He shrugged. "She can tell you all about it."

As they handed out toys to the delighted children, Carrie tried to envision May as one of the small girls who stood before her. True, the children seemed happy enough, but. . . how could May be so happy and peaceful after growing up in an orphanage? What had happened to her parents? Carrie had a hundred questions to ask by the time she and Charles pulled up in front of the Tanner house.

She bounded into May's room, catching herself just as she bent to give the elderly woman a hug. What was she doing? Embarrassed, she dropped into a chair. "The children send their love, May."

The older woman's eyes glowed. "Tell me all about it, please," she scribbled quickly.

Carrie related every detail, enjoying the joy on May's face. "Thank you for letting me be a part of your 'Blessing Day,' May," she said seriously. "It was a wonderful experience."

May nodded, pointing to a hand-stitched sampler that hung above her bed.

" 'It is more blessed to give than to receive,' " Carrie read out loud. "I guess I have to agree with that. Today, at least." Getting up, she started out of the room. At the doorway, she turned back to May hesitantly. "Would you tell me about growing up at the orphanage?"

May raised her eyebrows in surprise, but nodded her head. She wrote briefly on the tablet, then handed it to Carrie.

"Didn't your mother tell you about it?"

The words leapt out at Carrie. She read them again, certain she was misunderstanding. Still the words made no sense, and she frowned at May. "What are you talking about?"

May stared at her in consternation, then snatched the tablet. "Didn't you know your mother and I grew up together at that orphanage?"

"My. . .mother?" It had been so long since she had spoken the hated word.

May cocked her head, giving Carrie a searching look. Grasping her pen, she wrote furiously for several minutes while Carrie sat in stunned silence.

Carrie had never known much about her mother; she had never cared to. But how did May know who Carrie's mother was? Carrie sat straight up in her chair. May knew who her mother was! Then. . .the Tanners knew who she, Carrie, really was. She stole a glance at May.

Zach's mother finished writing and held the tablet out to Carrie.

She took it with a trembling hand, not sure she wanted to know what was written. She glanced up and caught May's compassionate gaze. Somehow that look gave her courage. She took a deep breath.

"Carrie, I'm sorry I surprised you. I thought you knew that I knew your mother. Don't feel bad, dear. Nothing can change the fact that I love you."

Carrie felt the tears beginning to prick her eyes. She blinked them away and kept reading.

"Your mother and I arrived at the orphanage about the

same time. I remember her so well. She was such a sad little thing. I was sad, too; my grandmother had just died. But Rachel was different." Carrie brushed away her tears. *Rachel. My mother's name was Rachel,* she thought as her eyes returned to the page. "Rumor had it that she had parents; they just didn't want her. At least the rest of us had known the love of a parent for a while."

Carrie paused. Her mother had been an unwanted child? It was hard to feel compassion for her long-despised mother, yet. . . . She turned back to the tablet.

"I never did know Rachel too well, Carrie. She kept to herself and turned away all attempts at friendship. Finally, everyone left her alone.

"When I was eighteen, I moved out of the orphanage. Soon after, I married a wonderful man named Thaddeus Green."

Carrie smiled in recognition. She remembered the name from Zach's Bible.

"Thaddeus and I moved to Bailey almost right away. We had lived there about a year when I saw Rachel in town one day. I hardly recognized her and she turned away when she saw me. I learned a few days later why she was there and the name she called herself. I tried to talk to her, but she wouldn't see me—didn't want anyone to know who she really was, I guess. I never stopped praying for her, though, and was sorry when I heard of her death."

Carrie laid the tablet down. She bowed her head, letting the tears fall unheeded. "How can you be so nice to me, knowing who—what I am?" Her voice was hoarse as she looked up at May. "Do you know what I am? What she made me into?" Carrie's voice rose to a shout, the years of bitterness pouring out in great waves. "She made me into what she was. If only she would have let me remain an innocent little girl!" The anger spent itself at last, and Carrie's voice broke in anguish.

"If only she had loved me. . . ." Carrie started as she felt May's arms around her. Somehow May had managed to inch her way over to where Carrie sat, and now she held the younger woman tightly to her breast.

The last of the dam gave way then, and Carrie sobbed into May's shoulder. Gradually, the sobs stilled as Charles' voice filled the room. His voice was not loud, but the sudden peace that flowed into the room was enough to touch Carrie deeply.

"Father God, I pray that You would touch this dear young woman with Your love," she heard him pray. "Let her know somehow that You can give her the peace and love that she longs for so deeply."

❧

Carrie sat up for a long time that evening, staring into the blackness of the night. Her body felt like lead, yet sleep refused to come.

You must forgive your mother, Carrie, or you will never know true peace. Pastor Dan's long-ago words came back to Carrie's mind, causing her to squirm. After all, her mother was dead—what did it matter if Carrie forgave her or not? Still, the image of a small sad girl abandoned at an orphanage filled Carrie's weary mind as she sought the refuge of sleep.

Thoughts of her mother haunted her for days, leaving Carrie restless and irritable. May watched with silent compassion. Finally, Charles suggested an outing.

"I think the weather is nice enough to take May out for a few hours, don't you, Nurse Carrie?" Charles winked at her.

Carrie readily agreed, and it was decided that they would have a picnic after attending the morning service at church. Until now, Carrie had politely declined Charles' invitations to attend church with him; but with May going, how could she refuse?

May's eyes shone with tears of joy as Charles carried her into the tiny church. Friends and neighbors flocked around her, happy to see their old friend. Carrie trailed behind uncertainly until Charles introduced her. She was immediately besieged with warm smiles and welcoming handshakes.

At least I can't say these people aren't friendly, Carrie mused as she slipped into the pew beside May. The older woman reached over and squeezed her hand tightly. Carrie patted the gnarled fingers affectionately. "How long has it been since you've been here, May?" she whispered.

Zach's mother struggled to hold up four fingers.

"Four months?"

May nodded, then turned her attention to the front as the organ sounded.

Carrie settled back with a sigh, determined for May's sake to at least act interested. Her thoughts flew to Pastor Dan as the minister began to speak, and she had to fight back a sudden wave of homesickness. How good it would be to see Pastor Dan and Sister Louisa again.

She jerked her attention back to the present as Charles handed her a huge Bible. Carrie stared at it blankly for a moment until she realized that the minister was announcing his text. Surreptitiously watching as Charles opened his own Bible, Carrie turned to the passage in Matthew 27 without much trouble. As the young pastor began to read about Jesus' arrest and trial, Carrie realized that next Sunday was Easter. *He must be building up to next week's sermon,* she thought. She had heard the story numerous times and was following along half-listening when the minister suddenly stopped.

"Did you hear that verse?" His gaze seemed to be on her face. "Let me read it again: Verse twenty-two says, 'Pilate saith unto them, What shall I do then with Jesus which is called Christ?' " His eyes roamed slowly over the congregation. "I believe that this is a question each one of us must answer today. What will *you* do with Jesus who is called Christ?"

Carrie felt a brief moment of panic. *Surely the preacher wasn't speaking to me, Carrie Winthrop. . . .*

"Everyone must make a decision at some point in their life. Some will make it sooner, some later; but everyone will ultimately decide whether to accept or reject Jesus Christ."

Carrie fidgeted on the hard pew. *Why did Charles have to pick today for the picnic anyway?* She cast a suspicious glance at him, but he appeared to be listening intently.

"You may think you can put the decision off; and perhaps you can for a while. But you will never have any peace until you face the question."

Carrie felt her face begin to burn.

"Jesus Christ is the only truth, the only peace, the only joy. He came to free you from your sin and pain. What will you do with Him? What will you do with Jesus Christ?"

Carrie pressed her legs together tightly to stop them from shaking. Willing herself to sit still, she deliberately turned her attention from the powerful words being spoken. They reminded her too much of Zach's words that day at the waterfall. *God loves you. . .wants to heal you. . .*

Staring out the window, she concentrated on thoughts of spring and sunshine until at last the sermon was over. She heaved a sigh of relief, glad that May hadn't seemed to notice her profound discomfort.

૨૦

The picnic went well despite Carrie's troubling morning. They all ate too much food, reminding Carrie once again of her picnic with Zach. May's cheeks took on a rosy glow from the fresh air and laughter. Carrie was delighted that her patient was doing so well, but insisted that May rest as soon as they arrived home.

"You musn't get overtired," she said as she tucked Zach's mother into bed. "I'll check on you in an hour or so."

Carrie kept herself occupied all day, knowing the path her thoughts would take if she had time to think. All too soon evening came. Charles and May bid her good night, and Carrie was left alone with her thoughts.

What will you do with this Jesus called Christ? Even though she knew it was coming, the question hit her with the force of a lead weight.

eleven

"Surely goodness and mercy shall follow me all the days of my life: and I will dwell in the house of the Lord for ever."

Zach's eyes flew open as the woman's voice paused. "Louisa," he croaked.

The elderly woman jumped, her hand going to her throat. "Goodness, Zach! You startled me. How are you feeling?"

Zach considered the question. "Hungry."

Sister Louisa chuckled. "I guess that answers my question well enough. You gave us quite a scare, you know."

Zach raised an eyebrow, wondering for the first time how he came to be in bed at Pastor Dan and Sister Louisa's house.

"Clarence Yeakley almost killed you."

Yeakley! Now he remembered. Clarence had jumped him as he walked home from the Parkers'. Zach groaned. "Did he get away?"

Louisa nodded, a grim expression marring her countenance. "I'm afraid so, Zach. There were several witnesses, but he ran before anyone could grab him."

Zach gingerly probed his swollen face with practiced fingers. "Not too often the doctor has to treat himself," he joked, fervently wishing for Carrie's gentle touch. He could almost feel her cool fingers on his forehead, her comforting voice. . . . "I'm going home, Louisa," he said suddenly.

"I think that's a wonderful idea, Dr. Tanner." She patted his arm and rose to her feet. "Yes, I think that would be the best medicine for you, Zach," she said, almost to herself.

❧

Zach lingered in Bailey for a few days, letting his battered body heal. He soon felt like his old self, with only an occasional throbbing in his jaw to remind him of the unpleasant incident. After promising that he would be back in a week, he eagerly boarded the train that would take him to three pairs of open arms—well, two at least. He wasn't sure how Carrie would react. He prayed she would be glad to see him.

❧

Zach strode off the train, scanning the crowd for Charles' tall figure. Suddenly he was clasped from behind in a hearty bear hug.

"Good to have you home, son."

The words almost brought tears to Zach's eyes. He hadn't realized how much he had missed the supportive love of his parents.

"I didn't tell the girls you were coming," Charles explained as Zach loaded his trunk in the wagon. "I thought maybe we'd surprise them."

Zach smiled at his father's casual use of the word "girls." *Carrie must be fitting into the family just fine,* he mused.

"How is Mama?"

Charles glanced at his son. "Pretty well, Zach. She sure took to that pretty little nurse you sent us."

Zach frowned at the forced cheeriness of his father's words. "Is she any better?"

"If you mean Carrie, yes, she's much better. But as for your mama. . ." He heaved a sigh. "I don't know, Zach," he said heavily. "Sometimes she seems to be doing better, then other times. . . ." His voice trailed off again.

The silence stretched on. Both men stared at the horses as they plodded along.

"I'm worried about her, Zach," Charles said finally. "Sometimes I don't think I'll have her with me much longer."

Zach started. Surely it wasn't that bad. "I'll check her while I'm home," he promised.

Charles nodded, blinking back the moisture that had gathered in his eyes.

"Well, here we are, Zach," Charles said a few minutes later. "I'll wager there's two ladies that'll be mighty glad to see you."

Zach gazed up at the windows of the familiar house. "I hope so," he murmured. "I hope so."

☙

Zach could hear her low voice as he paused by his mother's open door. Unobserved, he watched the two women. Carrie sat near May's bed, her head bent over the book she was reading. May listened intently, her hands lying limp in her lap.

Suddenly Carrie glanced up, and Zach's heart skipped a beat. How beautiful she was! Her lovely copper hair was done in a looser, more becoming style, and she had on a dress that enhanced her natural beauty. But the welcoming smile on her lips was all Zach saw. Holding his arms out silently, his heart thrilled as she came willingly into his embrace.

Gazing at his mother over Carrie's shoulder, he was glad to see an approving glint in her eye.

☙

Carrie pulled away, her face flaming. How could she have thrown herself at him like that?

"Hello, Carrie," Zach said softly.

"Zach." She backed away from him. "You surprised me." Her words sounded lame even to her own ears.

Zach chuckled. Drawing her to his side, he gave her a quick squeeze. "I see you're taking good care of my mother, Nurse Carrie." Zach bent to kiss May's cheek. "How are you, Mama?" he asked tenderly.

She pressed his hand and nodded, her eyes expressing her joy. She reached for her tablet.

"How long can you stay?" Carrie read May's question out loud, her own eyes asking the same.

"Oh, long enough for you to wish I was gone," he teased. "About a week."

A week! Carrie's heart leapt. She had been missing him so dreadfully, and now he was here for a whole week! She smiled at him shyly. The look he gave her in return made her flush, and she turned away in embarrassment, fiddling with May's covers.

"Carrie, do you think you could fix a weary traveler something to eat?"

Carrie glanced at May. Her eyes twinkled with delight as she looked from Zach to Carrie and gave a slight nod.

✿

Carrie set the heaping plate in front of Zach. "You must be starved," she commented. She had had time to gain her composure as Zach visited with his father, and now she was eager to talk to him.

She studied him out of the corner of her eye as he ate, reacquainting herself with his gentle eyes, his strong hands. . . . How she had missed him! It seemed like years since the day he had kissed her at the waterfall. . . .

"Thank you, Carrie. That was wonderful." Zach's voice startled her out of her reverie, and she stared blankly at him for a moment before noticing his empty plate.

"You're welcome," she murmured, embarrassed that he had caught her daydreaming. "Can I get you anything else?"

"You could come out and sit on the porch with me."

Charles still sat at the table nursing a cup of coffee. He grinned as Carrie cast a questioning glance at him. "Run along, you two. I'll take May her supper."

Carrie slowly untied her apron strings. She had dreamed about Zach for so long, but now that the moment was finally here she was suddenly shy.

"Come on, Carrie. We have a lot of catching up to do."

✿

The smell of honeysuckle was heavy in the still evening air, and Carrie could hear the clink of dishes in the kitchen as Charles prepared a tray for his wife. She took a deep breath, daring to meet Zach's expectant gaze.

He patted the seat next to him on the swing. "Come sit with me."

She obeyed nervously. Now that they were alone, what would she say? The look in Zach's dark eyes as he smiled at her did nothing to calm the sudden churning of her stomach.

"Mama looks wonderful. You must be taking good care of her."

Carrie shrugged. "She was a little bit anemic. I've been giving her a tincture of yellow dock twice a day—"

"Tell me what has happened to you, Carrie." His voice was soft.

"What do you mean?" Something *had* happened, but surely it wasn't that obvious.

"There's something different about you." He touched her cheek lightly with one finger. "Your new hairstyle and pretty dress are very becoming, but there's something different in your eyes that is even more beautiful to me than any dress."

Carrie's pulse began to race at the intimate tone of Zach's voice. "I finally accepted the fact that God is love, and that He really does loves me," she said quietly. "It's made all the difference in the world. I have peace now."

He squeezed her hand. "How did it happen?"

Her eyes filled with tears as she spoke of her days of struggle. "I just couldn't deny the question of what to do with Jesus, Zach. It rang in my head constantly, and I knew I would never have peace until I faced the truth." She looked up at him. "Your mother was such a help to me, Zach. It was through her and Charles' love that I realized God's love." She shook her head. "I couldn't believe that they still loved me, knowing who I was."

"I know someone else who loves you, Carrie." Zach's voice was tender as he gazed into her eyes.

She sat frozen, afraid to hope.

He pulled her to him slowly, pressing her head to his chest. "Ah, Carrie." He sighed. "I've loved you for so long."

She was stunned. Could it really be true? She snuggled down into the warmth of his arms, a deep sense of happiness flooding over her. "Are you sure?" she murmured.

He chuckled a deep rumbling chuckle, and Carrie thrilled at the happy sound. "I'm positive." Pushing her away an inch, he looked down at her tenderly. "Can I believe what I see written in your eyes, Carrie? Do you love me?"

She felt her cheeks grow rosy as she nodded. "I do love you, Zach," she whispered.

He smiled then, drawing her face to his with gentle hands. The kiss was long and achingly sweet, putting to rest the last of her fears. Carrie pulled away first, gazing at him in wonder. "Why do you love me, Zach?"

His laughter rang out into the still night. "I hope I have a long time to figure that out, angel."

Carrie smiled in the darkness. "Me, too."

twelve

Carrie hummed softly as she plumped the pillows on May's bed. Zach loved her! She could still hardly believe it.

The clock in the hall gonged, startling her. *Zach should be bringing his mother back inside any time now.* Carrie frowned at the thought. May tired so easily these days. Of course, the fresh air would probably help her as much as anything.

She quickly straightened the pile of books on the invalid's bedside table. Placing May's well-used writing tablet on the top of the pile, Carrie was immediately curious as her own name caught her eye.

"No, absolutely not, Charles. I will not ruin Carrie's happiness," Carrie read. Obviously, May and Charles had been arguing about something. But how could May possibly ruin Carrie's happiness? Everything had been so wonderful last night.

"Carrie and I have an announcement to make," Zach had said proudly. "We're going to get married!"

Carrie blushed as Charles gave her a great bear hug. "Welcome to the family, little lady!" He turned to his wife. "Of course, she's already like a daughter to us, isn't she, May?"

Zach's mother had nodded, happy tears glistening in her eyes. She hugged Carrie to her as tightly as her feeble arms would allow, and even without words, Carrie knew she had finally gained a loving mother.

Carrie glanced back down at the tablet. "What they don't know won't hurt them, Charles," she read, frowning. What could May possibly be talking about? Carrie wrinkled her brow. Then in a sudden, sickening moment, she knew. That specialist that had come to see May last week! He must have found that May was worse than everyone thought.

Carrie laid the tablet down sorrowfully. *Dear, sweet May.*

She must be planning on keeping this a secret from Zach and me so we won't change our wedding plans.

Suddenly hearing voices, she stepped away from the tell-tale tablet. She was busily dusting when Zach carried May in.

"Well, how was your outing?" she asked, forcing cheeriness into her voice.

Zach grinned at her. "I'd hardly call fifteen minutes on the porch swing an outing, but I enjoyed it anyway. Didn't we, Mama?"

May nodded vigorously, her eyes sparkling.

Carrie smiled at May's pink cheeks and bright eyes. *She certainly didn't look any worse. . . .*

"Are you ready to go shopping, my love? We'd better let Mama get some rest."

Carrie blushed a deep crimson. It still startled her to hear Zach call her such things. She followed him out the door. "I'll be back in a bit, May. Are you sure you don't need anything from the store?"

❧

The shopping trip was successful, and Carrie came home with enough calico for three new dresses. She excitedly showed May her purchases while Zach looked on approvingly. "She'll be the prettiest doctor's wife around, don't you think so, Mama?"

Carrie rolled her eyes. "I'll be the *only* doctor's wife around Bailey, Zach."

He laughed. "Still the prettiest, though. I bet the townspeople won't even recognize you."

A strange look crossed Carrie's face. "Why not?" she whispered.

Zach failed to notice the warning signs. "Because you're such a fancy lady now," he teased.

Carrie blanched, and behind her, May was shaking her head frantically.

Zach reached for Carrie as she rushed from the room, but she shook off his hand. Slumping down in the chair, Zach stared at his mother. "I didn't realize," he said slowly.

May picked up her tablet. "Be patient with her, Zach. She's come a long way, but her wounds are still healing."

Zach rubbed the back of his neck. "I guess I thought she was over trying to be the opposite of her mother."

May shook her head slowly. "It's going to take time, son," she wrote. "But she's on the right path. Just love her."

"I will, Mama." Zach smiled at her. "I can't help it."

•≥

Carrie sank down on the bed, trembling. *Stop it,* she scolded herself. *You're overreacting.* Lying back on the bed, she stared at the ceiling. *Zach's going to think you're a fool.*

Why couldn't she just forget about her mother? She frowned. It just wasn't that easy. Slowly, her whirling thoughts settled. Reaching for her Bible, Carrie found the now-familiar passage in 2 Corinthians: "Therefore if any man be in Christ, he is a new creature: old things are passed away; behold, all things are become new."

Thank You, Father, she breathed. *Thank You for doing away with the old, and making me new. I'm sorry I forget sometimes. Thank You for always being there. . . .*

She awoke the next morning feeling refreshed. She had won another victory over her fears. She jumped up and opened the curtains, delighted as the brilliant sunshine flooded the room. Zach would be leaving tomorrow, but he would be back in a few weeks to get her. Then they would be married!

Carrie hugged herself. It was just too perfect! Pastor Dan would do the ceremony, and even May and Charles were going to make the trip to Bailey for the big event.

She smiled at her reflection in the mirror. *Who would have thought I would be marrying Zach Tanner?* she mused. Giving her hair one final pat, she bustled out to the kitchen.

"Good morning, Carrie." Zach's voice was hesitant.

Carrie glanced at him, dismayed as she realized he must think she was angry with him. Setting down the coffee pot, she placed both hands on his cheeks. "I'm sorry about yesterday,

Zach. I wasn't angry with you, I was just—"

Her words stopped abruptly as Zach lowered his lips to hers. He kissed her tenderly, kindling an alarming response in Carrie. Pushing her away gently, he held her chin in his hand. "You don't have to say another word about it, Carrie. I'm sorry, too. I just wasn't thinking."

She smiled up at him. "Kiss me again."

The sound of a discreet cough directly behind her made Carrie jump out of Zach's embrace. She whirled around, finding herself looking into Charles' amused eyes.

"I guess the coffee's not ready yet," he said dryly.

"Some things are more important than coffee, Papa." Zach grinned at his father. "Why don't you go join Mama. Carrie and I will bring breakfast in to you two."

Charles chuckled. "Trying to get rid of me, are you?" He made his way to his wife's room, then turned. "Just don't take too long, or I'll come see what's keeping you."

Carrie giggled at the look on Zach's face as he drew her into his arms once again. "You aren't being very obedient to your father, Dr. Tanner."

"You taste much better than breakfast, Nurse Carrie," he murmured, ignoring her words.

❧

Quite a while later, Carrie took four empty coffee cups back to the kitchen. How she loved being part of this family! It was wonderful to know that there were good, kind men like Zach and Charles. Carrie grew pensive as she rinsed the cups. What could her life have been like if she had grown up with a loving father like Charles? Though her nightmares had all but ceased, Carrie now found her conscious thoughts turning toward her mother and father more than she would have liked.

She felt she was making real progress on forgiving her mother, but as for her father. . . . How could she forgive someone when she didn't even know who he was? Up until recently, she had been content to let her father remain anonymous. True, she had yearned for a father's love her entire life, but had never really associated a nameless, faceless man with love.

Could her father be out there somewhere? Would he want her—love her? Did he even know she existed? She shook her head. What if she were to find him and he turned out to be a horrible person? She sighed. It was too big of a decision to make lightly. Perhaps after she and Zach were married she would have the strength to do it. Until then. . . She smiled lovingly at Zach as he entered the kitchen, her heart suddenly dancing again. In just a few weeks, she would belong to him forever.

thirteen

"We'll see you in a few weeks!"

Carrie waved at Charles and May one last time, then turned to Zach. "I can't believe that we'll be married in five weeks!"

Zach smiled down at her, putting his hand out for her valise. "If we miss this train, we might still be here in five weeks!" He glanced anxiously at the huffing train. "Never did care for these steaming monsters," Carrie heard him mutter.

Suppressing a grin, she boarded the train in front of him. Settling in her seat, she sighed contentedly. Soon they would be home.

The sudden tears that came to her eyes as they steamed into Bailey surprised her. "I hadn't realized how much I missed this place," she murmured softly.

Zach nodded. "I know what you mean. Sometimes we don't appreciate things or people until we haven't had them for a while." He gave her a meaningful look, and Carrie blushed. It felt good to know that Zach had missed her those weeks they had been apart.

"Oh, Zach, I'm so glad to see you!" The high-pitched voice crashed into Carrie's pleasant thoughts. Turning toward the source, she was irritated to see Annabelle Parker, her arm looped possessively through Zach's.

"Hello, Carrie," Annabelle said brightly. "It's good to have you back."

"Hello, Annabelle." Carrie flicked a questioning glance at Zach. He shrugged slightly.

Carrie turned to collect her bags, frowning. Whatever had been going on in Bailey these months she had been gone? Surely everyone knew by now that she and Zach were getting married.

"Carrie." Zach's calm voice stilled her tumbling thoughts. "I'm sorry. I know what that must have looked like to you."

Carrie glanced up. Annabelle was nowhere to be seen.

Zach sighed, pulling Carrie down beside him on a bench. "Annabelle Parker means nothing to me, Carrie. She's like that with all the men." He touched her cheek gently. "You're the only woman for me."

Carrie's blue eyes reflected her relief. "I thought maybe—"

"Hush. Don't think about it any more. I love you." Zach's voice was gentle, yet firm. "I will always love only you."

Zach's words rang in Carrie's mind for days. *I will always love you. . .love you. . .only you.* Between wedding preparations and medical emergencies, Carrie saw very little of Zach for the first week they were back in town, but his words of love sustained her. They had decided that Zach would move into Carrie's house once they were married, so on top of everything else, Carrie worked long hours sewing new curtains and quilts. It hardly seemed like work, so great was her anticipation of the time that Zach would truly share life with her in all senses of the word.

Sister Louisa and Pastor Dan had been elated at the news of the upcoming wedding. Often the elderly pastor's wife would sit up with Carrie far into the night as together they sewed the beautiful wedding dress.

"Oh, Louisa," Carrie sighed one evening. "God has been so good to me."

Louisa's eyes sparkled. "It's wonderful to hear you say those words, Carrie. You don't know how I've prayed that you would find the peace that comes from Him."

Carrie nodded. "I'm thankful for your prayers, Louisa. I'm sure you were a great force in my coming to know Christ. I always knew you and Pastor Dan loved me and were praying for me, no matter what was happening."

The older woman smiled. "You're worth all those prayers, Carrie. You know we've loved you ever since you were a little girl and. . ." Louisa stopped, a strange expression crossing her face. "Did Zach ever tell you. . .?" she began, then stopped.

Carrie glanced up from threading the tiny pearl beads. "Did he ever tell me what?"

"Oh, never mind. Hand me some more of that lace, will you please?"

Carrie obeyed Louisa's request, a puzzled frown on her face. Was there something Zach needed to tell her? Louisa was already talking about a new pie recipe, and Carrie nodded mechanically as she continued to wonder at the older woman's words. *Surely if whatever it was was important, Zach has already told me,* she decided. Carefully stringing another pearl onto her thread, Carrie thought no more of Louisa's comment until weeks later.

ﾊ

The incessant rain pounding on her roof had lulled Carrie into a deep, dreamless sleep. Exhausted by the past weeks, she slept soundly through the deep, rumbling thunder and cracking lightning.

"Carrie!" Zach's frantic voice suddenly broke through to her consciousness. She jumped from the bed, pulling on her robe. Jerking open the door, she was horrified to see Zach standing in ankle-deep water where her porch should have been.

"Thank God you're safe," he murmured, pulling her to him for the briefest of moments. Releasing her, his voice tensed again. "Crow Creek is flooding. It's going to be bad." At the look on her face, he smiled at her slightly. "God will protect us, Carrie."

Carrie nodded mutely. How had this happened so quickly? It had been raining when she went to sleep, but this. . .

"Carrie! Get your coat on. We've got to hurry, love."

Zach's voice finally prodded her into action. Flying around the room, she swiftly gathered a few keepsakes. Stuffing them into a bag, she snatched her coat and hat. *Good-bye, house,* she said silently as she ran for the barn.

Zach had already untied Pepper. The big horse whinnied in fear as Zach freed Molasses. "It's going to be all right, Pepper," Zach crooned.

As she hurriedly pushed her bag into Pepper's saddlebag, Carrie noted with dismay that the water here in the barn was already above her ankles. Grasping the horse's lead, she headed for the door.

"I need to get my other bag." She had to shout against the rising wind. "Wait for me."

She snatched her supply bag from the hall table, the warmth of her small house beckoning her to curl up by the fire where it was safe. Shaking the selfish thought from her mind, she joined Zach outside. "I'm ready."

She was unprepared for the sight that met her eyes as they neared town. People ran desperately toward the higher ground, carrying children and belongings.

"Don't waste your time going down there, Doc," one man yelled as he rushed passed. "Everything is gone."

Zach urged Pepper on. "We've got to see if anyone down there needs help, Carrie."

She nodded. "I'm going to check to make sure Widow Greyson is all right first. I'll catch up to you."

"I'll meet you at the O'Reillys' house," he shouted over the storm.

"God go with you, Zach."

"And you." He smiled at her, then disappeared into the driving rain.

Carrie turned toward the tiny house where Widow Greyson lived on the edge of town. *At least Molasses can still wade through easily enough,* she thought grimly, surveying the swirling water.

"Mrs. Greyson!" Carrie called loudly, but heard no response. Hopefully someone had already helped the elderly woman to higher ground, but if not. . . Carrie pressed her lips together, her thoughts and prayers becoming as one. Seeing the door ajar, she pushed her way into the small house. Surely someone had remembered Widow Greyson.

The water had already begun to climb up to the seats of the chairs. Sweeping the room with a swift glance, Carrie's heart jumped as she saw the old woman trembling on the tiny bed, her eyes tightly closed as if to block out her fear. "Mrs. Greyson!"

The elderly woman cried out in relief as she saw Carrie. "I thought for sure I was gonna drown, honey," she said over and over. "The good Lord musta sent ya."

Carrie smiled, trying to keep the urgency out of her voice. "I'm sure He did, Mrs. Greyson. Now, can you hang onto my neck while I help you off the bed?"

❧

What seemed to be hours later, Carrie led Molasses up the hill to the O'Reillys' barn, arriving dripping and exhausted.

Eager hands reached to take her shivering burden, and Carrie relaxed instantly when she heard Zach's voice above the others. Snuggling into his arms, she felt as warm as if she were in front of the fire.

"Good work, nurse," he murmured into her hair. "Now, let's get you warmed up."

❧

Carrie stood with her hands on her hips, surveying her once beautiful house and yard. *I should be thankful I still have a house,* she thought, sighing. So many others who had lived in and around town had left the shelter of the O'Reillys' barn only to find that they had no home. *I should be thankful.* Still, she sighed again. The wedding was only two weeks away, and everything in sight was covered with mud.

She kicked at the ground in disgust, then straightened her shoulders resolutely. *You're not going to get a thing done if you don't start somewhere,* she told herself sternly. *Now, get going!*

Hours later, she gazed around her in satisfaction. The parlor and kitchen gleamed like new. "That's enough for one day, don't you think so, Toby?"

The little dog cocked his head in agreement, and Carrie patted him as she wearily walked to the bedroom. *Zach will be here soon for supper, and—* Glimpsing herself in the mirror, Carrie had to laugh at her mud-covered features. *I'd better wash up quick, or Zach won't recognize me!*

Still smiling, she peeled off her filthy clothes. She poured the water that had been heating into the bathtub, added a sachet of lavender, then eased into the scented water with a grateful sigh. As her aching muscles relaxed, her mind drifted to the upcoming wedding. *In just two weeks I'll be Mrs. Tanner,* she thought happily. *Thank You, Father. You've blessed me so much. . . .*

fourteen

Zach rubbed the back of his neck wearily. Thank God there had been only minor injuries to treat after the flood, but there was so much work to be done! When he wasn't tending to a patient, Zach worked alongside the rest of the townspeople, trying to put their devastated town back together. Some of the buildings had been completely swept away, but others like the sheriff's office where Zach was working only needed a thorough cleaning.

Bending to retrieve his broom, Zach knocked a stack of damp papers to the floor. He picked them up hastily. Spreading them out on the desk to dry, the name at the top of one of the documents caught his eye. He picked it up without thinking, and at first, his mind refused to grasp the significance of what he held in his hands. Slowly the truth dawned on him. Dropping the paper as if it were a poisonous snake, the young doctor buried his face in his hands. "No! It can't be! No!"

❧

"Zach, it's Pastor Dan. Open the door." The elderly minister pounded on Zach's door once again. "Come on, son. I know you're in there."

Sighing, Zach got to his feet and shuffled to the door.

Dan gaped at the haggard figure that stood before him. "May I come in?"

The younger man nodded listlessly, motioning to a chair.

"What is this all about, son?" Pastor Dan peered anxiously at Zach. "Carrie said you never showed up for supper last night, and Mrs. Granger says you haven't come out of this room since yesterday afternoon. Are you ill?"

"Why didn't you and Louisa tell me, Dan?" The pain in Zach's voice was so thick it made the old minister wince.

"Tell you what, Zach?" A tiny spark of dread touched the pastor's eyes.

"This." Zach shoved a water-stained paper in front of Pastor Dan's bewildered eyes. "Surely you knew."

Pastor Dan read the paper reluctantly, blanching as he saw the two signatures at the bottom. "Zach, I—" He stopped, compassion sweeping his features as he continued in a gentle tone. "We didn't know, Zach. Yes, of course we knew what your father was *accused* of—the whole town knew; but Louisa and I didn't believe it. We still don't." He shook his head. "I know you don't remember your father much, Zach, but he was a fine Christian man. He loved you and your mother as much as a man could love his family."

"What are you saying, Dan? That my father was too virtuous to have fathered a child with a. . .a prostitute?"

Pastor Dan stared at Zach for a long moment. "No, Zach. Only God knows a man's heart. All I can say is that the Thaddeus Green I knew would never do such a thing."

"Maybe you didn't really know him."

The man of God sighed heavily. "Maybe not, Zach. It does seem that you have indisputable evidence here," he said sadly, indicating the telltale document he still held in his hand.

Zach stared out the window. "What am I going to tell Carrie? What?" His voice rose as he whirled to stare at the pastor. "What am I going to say to her, Dan? I can't very well walk up to her and say, 'I'm sorry, Carrie. We can't get married because you're my sister.' " He slumped onto the bed. "The father she never knew was my father. I didn't know God could be so cruel."

"Zach—"

"I don't want to hear it, Dan." Zach turned his back on his old friend.

❧

Mrs. Granger appeared at her door, sleepy-eyed and terse. "What is so important at this late hour, Dr. Tanner?"

"I'm sorry to disturb you, Mrs. Granger, but I'm leaving for Denver—"

"*Now?*" She wrinkled her brow curiously. "What is going on, young man? You've been acting awful strange."

"I've got to find an answer and it can't wait." He turned and left the bewildered woman staring after him.

❧

Zach sat slumped in the saddle, the steep road blurring in front of his weary eyes. Too impatient to wait for the morning train to Denver, Zach had stolen into the barn at Carrie's last night and managed to saddle Pepper without awakening Toby. Now in the gray light of predawn, his hours of hard riding were catching up with him. Images of Carrie rose in his mind unbidden. How he longed to feel her in his arms, to know that soon she would be his. . . . *Get ahold of yourself, Tanner,* he ordered. *All you have left of Carrie now are just dreams and memories, unless. . .*

Pepper cantered wearily up to the Tanners' front door. Zach slid off the horse, burying his face in Pepper's side for a long moment. "God, I can't face this—"

The front door creaked open. Zach glanced up, startled.

"How did you know to come, son?" Charles Tanner's usually buoyant voice was dull.

"What do you mean? I—" Zach's heart suddenly felt heavy with dread. "It's Mama, isn't it?" he whispered.

Charles nodded silently. Zach rushed up to the porch where his stepfather stood, taking the older man into his arms as if he were a child. Charles cried deep, wrenching sobs as he felt the strong arms of his son. "She's gone, Zach," he whispered finally. "Gone."

In a daze, Zach led Charles over to the porch swing. "Tell me what happened, Papa. Did she suddenly worsen?"

Charles dried his eyes. "No, no, nothing like that. In fact, I think she was doing better. She just—oh, Zach, I'm ashamed to tell you."

"Tell me, Papa," Zach commanded gently. "It's all right."

"She wanted to see the children at the orphanage, Zach. For weeks she had been begging me to take her." Charles' eyes pleaded with Zach for understanding. "I finally gave in and took her over there for a few hours. You should have seen the happiness on her face as she handed out those little toys of hers to the children." He stopped, remembering.

"Go on, Papa."

Charles started, as if he had forgotten Zach's presence. "She seemed a bit tired when we got home, but insisted she felt fine. A few days later she woke up with funny little bumps all over her and. . ."

Zach moaned.

"Oh, Zach. I didn't know! I never would have taken her there if I would've known that some of the children had just had the measles." Charles was trembling. "It was just too much for her in her weakened condition."

Zach gazed compassionately at the man he had called father for so long. Suddenly, Zach was the parent and Charles the hurting child. He placed his hand gently on Charles' shoulder. "It wasn't your fault, Papa," he said quietly. "You didn't know." Standing up heavily, he entered the silent house.

❧

Zach lay motionless on the bed, staring at the ceiling. He had tried to pray, but the words wouldn't come. Mama was gone. Gone! And gone with her was the answer to the question that could change Zach's life forever. He pounded the pillow. Why couldn't she have told him? Surely he was man enough to handle the truth. Now the only people who could ease his pain were dead—gone forever.

God, I can't go on like this! I can't live my whole life without Carrie, wondering if she really is my sister! God, I love her! I thought You sent her to me. . . .

He awoke hours later with a raging headache. Stumbling out to the kitchen, he almost tripped over Charles.

Charles turned from the darkened window with a sad smile.

"You couldn't sleep either, eh, Zach?"

Zach shook his head. "I'm used to it. Haven't slept in days."

Charles gave him an odd look. "I never did ask you why you came home. You surely didn't have time to receive my telegram. I just sent it last night."

"No, I didn't get the telegram. I came to. . .to ask Mama a question."

Charles eased down into a chair. "Is it something I can help you with, son?" he asked cautiously.

Zach wiped his hand across his eyes with a weary sigh. "I would like to think so, but. . ." His words trailed off at the look on Charles' face. "You already know what I'm going to ask you, don't you?"

The older man nodded slowly. "I told May a hundred times if I told her once that it wasn't right to keep it a secret." He shook his head. "I guess she just thought what you didn't know wouldn't hurt you."

Zach jumped up, overturning his chair. "How could she think it wouldn't hurt me? She knew I loved Carrie!" He was shouting now, unable to stop the torrent of words. "Why did she let it happen? Did she think it was just going to work out fine if neither of us knew? I can't marry my half-sister!"

Charles stared at his stepson. "I think you've misunderstood, Zach. Your father was *accused* of fathering Carrie. Neither your mother nor I believe it to be true. Your father was a fine Christian man who loved his family." He gave Zach a hard look. "Your mother never wanted to tell you about it, not to harm you, but because it simply is not true."

Zach gaped at the assurance in Charles' voice. A faint gleam of hope lighted his eyes for a moment, then faded. "I saw his signature on the birth certificate," he said dully.

Charles looked momentarily startled, then shook his head. "I still don't believe it, Zach."

"But—"

"Let me tell you why. When Thaddeus and May were first

married, Thad worked at the general store there in Bailey. He discovered that the owner was cheating the folks, and went to the sheriff with it."

Zach frowned. "What does this have to do with Carrie?"

"I'm coming to that." Charles leaned back in his chair, taking a sip of his now-cold coffee. Grimacing, he set the cup down. "Your father made an enemy that day, Zach. When Yeakley found out that Thad had gone to the sheriff—"

"Yeakley!"

"Frank Yeakley. He was the owner of the general store at that time."

"Did he have a son named Clarence?"

Charles looked perplexed. "Well, I don't know, Zach. What does it matter?"

Zach's mind was racing. "There's a young man named Clarence Yeakley that has given Carrie some trouble from time to time. Do you suppose. . .?"

Charles raised his eyebrows. "I don't know, Zach. It seems unlikely, but you never can tell. All I know is that after Thad went to the sheriff, Yeakley roughed him up a time or two, threatening to run him out of town." He stared into his coffee cup, then looked up at Zach almost apologetically. "Right after that, Rachel was pregnant with Carrie. The news spread like wildfire, and soon your father's name was involved."

Zach gritted his teeth. "Are you saying my father was framed?"

"I'm positive of it. Thad protested his innocence loudly, but no one believed him except May and a few of his friends, myself included. Then shortly before Rachel gave birth to Carrie, Thad and May paid her a visit." He closed his eyes in pain. "I don't know exactly what they found out that day, but very soon afterwards, Thad was 'accidentally' killed."

Zach started. "He was. . .murdered? I was told he'd been killed while hunting. I assumed it was an accident!"

Charles nodded. "Thad *was* out hunting that day, but the shot that killed him was no accident. If I were a betting man,

I'd put money on it."

"How can you be so sure?"

Charles glanced away. "Do you know why we moved away from Bailey?"

Zach shook his head.

"Your father had been dead for several years, and the sheriff who had investigated his death was retiring. Your mother and I had been married for a while, and she encouraged me to run for sheriff."

Zach stared at his stepfather. "I didn't know that!"

Charles nodded. "There were a few of us in the town that had reason to suspect that the sheriff was not totally on the up-and-up. We had been observing him for some time. Anyway, I decided I could do the job right, with God's help." Charles stood up and began pacing restlessly. "Everything was going well, and it appeared I would be the next sheriff. Then a few days before the election, a man—a drifter—was murdered. I was accused of doing the deed."

"What?"

Charles smiled sadly. "No one had any proof, but the damage had been done. The doubt placed in the minds of the townsfolk was enough to tip the scales in favor of one of the retiring sheriff's cronies." He stopped pacing and stared directly at Zach. "You know what I think, Zach? If I were to become sheriff, I would have had access to a lot of confidential information. I think I was too close to finding out the truth about your father's death, and the sheriff knew it."

Zach gaped at Charles, suddenly recalling the snippets of conversations he had overheard as a child. "So that's why—that's what you and Mama were talking about," he said slowly. "I overheard you and Mama arguing one night about you being accused of something," he confessed to Charles. "I always wondered what it meant."

"Yes. I decided that it would be unfair to subject you and May to any more of the vicious gossip going on about me."

Zach sank back against the chair, his thoughts whirling. "If my father truly was innocent, then Carrie and I can—what about his signature on the birth certificate?"

"I'd say it was forged, son. Your father didn't commit adultery."

"That's what Pastor Dan said," Zach murmured, almost to himself. "If only I could find out for sure." Despair closed in on him once more. "I can't marry her until I'm sure, Papa. I just can't."

Charles nodded. "You'd better start praying then, Zach. Only God knows the whole truth."

Zach scowled at him. "I think God has done enough for me lately." His heart pricked him even as he said the words, but he refused to heed the still small voice. If this was the way God was going to treat him after all the years he had served Him, then maybe he'd just turn the tables. God could wait.

fifteen

"How could Zach just leave in the middle of the night without telling me?"

Toby cocked his head at Carrie as if trying to understand her distress.

"I hope something hasn't happened to May," Carrie worried out loud. "But Zach would have told me if it was something like that, wouldn't he?"

Realizing that she was pacing, Carrie let out a frustrated sigh. Maybe Pastor Dan and Sister Louisa knew where he went. Snatching her cape out of the closet, she ran to the barn. "At least he could have left me a note," she complained as she saddled Molasses.

❧

"Denver!" Carrie stared at Sister Louisa in consternation. "Did May take a turn for the worse?"

"Not that we know of, Carrie." Louisa darted a glance at her husband. "You say Zach left without talking to you?"

Carrie nodded. "It seems so unlike him. It worries me." She noticed the silent communication between the pastor and his wife. "What is it? Do you know why he left?"

Pastor Dan sighed. "Why don't you sit down, Carrie? There's something we must tell you."

"Dan, I don't think—"

"She has a right to know, Louisa."

Carrie sank down onto the nearest chair, her heart suddenly gripped with foreboding. "What is it?" she whispered.

Moments later, she sat stunned. "I can't believe it." All of her hopes and dreams. . .

"I *don't* believe it, Carrie." Louisa spoke firmly. "I don't believe for one second that Thaddeus Green was your father."

"But the signature on my birth certificate—"

"I think Zach will have the answers to all the questions after he talks to his mother," Pastor Dan said. "Why don't we just forget about it until he comes back?"

Carrie smiled at him wanly. "You're probably right, Pastor Dan. I'm sure everything will be fine." Her words sounded unconvincing, and Carrie took her leave a few minutes later.

She lay in bed, tears streaming down her cheeks. "Oh, Zach," she moaned over and over. "How can I live my life without you? I love you so much."

Toby snuggled closer, and Carrie hugged him to her tightly. "God, please help me to bear this," she sobbed. "I know that You love me. Please help me. . . ."

She drifted into a fitful sleep, awakening abruptly as an image of May's writing tablet forced itself into her thoughts. *No, absolutely not, Charles. I won't ruin Carrie's happiness.* Carrie recalled the words as if she had read them yesterday. *What they don't know won't hurt them. . . .* She let her breath out in a loud sigh. Could this have been what May was referring to?

She felt sure it was; yet how could May justify not telling them something so important? Carrie wrinkled her brow. *Surely May would know we would find out someday, unless. . . unless it wasn't true! That must be it!* May didn't think it was important to tell them about the accusation against Zach's father because it wasn't true. Carrie smiled.

Surely May would explain everything to Zach when he asked, and then they could get on with their lives. After all, the wedding was in only two weeks. Everything would be cleared up by then. Carrie snuggled back down under the covers, her heart light. "Come back to me soon, my love," she whispered sleepily. "I'm waiting for you."

❧

"I'm so sorry about May, Zach." Carrie gazed at him compassionately. In truth, her own heart ached over the loss of the loving woman who had become a mother to her. But this silent, grim Zach that had come back from Denver was not the man she knew and loved. He was in no state to give comfort to anyone. Of course, it was normal for him to grieve, but it somehow seemed to be more than that.

Carrie soon realized that Zach's visit to Denver had produced more questions than answers. She quietly put the wedding plans aside, knowing that she would wait for Zach as long as it took. Her fledgling faith remained strong, and she prayed daily that the truth would be revealed.

But as the days slipped into weeks with no answers, it became harder and harder to see each other daily, knowing what could have been. Carrie longed for the relationship they once had and often caught herself daydreaming about their life together.

"I can't go on like this, Carrie." Zach paced restlessly in front of the fireplace. "All I've been able to find out for sure is that Clarence Yeakley is Frank Yeakley's son."

He rubbed the back of his neck. "I'm sure they hold the key to all of this, but no one seems to know what happened to them. They couldn't have just vanished."

"Maybe we're overlooking someone who might be able to help us," Carrie suggested.

"There's no one left to ask, Carrie," Zach said in exasperation. "That's just it. Nobody here in Bailey or the surrounding towns is able or willing to give me any more information than I already have."

"I know that God is able—"

"I don't want to hear that, Carrie. If God was going to help us, He would've done it by now." He glared at her. "Maybe you don't really love me. You don't seem very upset about it."

Carrie was stunned by his accusation. "You don't know what you're saying, Zach. I'm just as anxious as you are to have this cleared up, but I'm trying not to let it ruin my whole life in the meantime."

"I can't help it. I thought God brought us together. I love you so much, and now He's taken you away from me. The

God I thought I knew isn't like that."

Carrie sighed. "It does seem that way sometimes, Zach. But I still believe God must have a reason—"

"I can't accept that, Carrie," Zach broke in harshly. "I've got to find the truth if it takes me the rest of my life." He grasped her shoulders in his intensity. "I'm leaving here, and I'm not coming back until I know."

Carrie gasped. "Zach, I—" Her words were stilled as he crushed her to him in a fervent embrace. His lips touched hers just long enough to ignite a raging fire before he thrust her from him with a groan. Heedless of the tears streaming down her face, he turned and walked away.

"God help me." Carrie heard his hoarse whisper as he stumbled blindly out the door.

sixteen

"I can't believe it's been six months since Zach left, Louisa." Carrie stared out the window. "I thought for sure. . . ." She let her words trail off into a sigh.

Louisa gazed at the younger woman, compassion evident in her old eyes. "I don't mean to pry, Carrie," she said hesitantly, "but do you have any plans?"

"Plans?"

"You can't spend the rest of your life waiting for Zach to come back," Louisa gently pointed out.

Carrie's shoulders slumped. "You're right, of course, Louisa," she admitted. "I just haven't wanted to face the thought of living without him."

"I didn't mean to suggest that you should give up all hope, dear," Louisa said hastily. "I know you still love him."

Carrie smiled sadly. "I will always love him. Nothing can ever change that. But you're right. I need to get on with my life."

"Forgive me if I sound presumptuous." Louisa's tone was uncharacteristically timid. "But have you ever considered getting any formal medical training?"

Carrie was startled. "Of course, I would love to, Louisa. But you know I don't have near enough money for that."

"If you had the money, would you go?" Louisa persisted.

"I would leave tomorrow." Carrie laughed, then sobered at the look on Louisa's face. "Why, you're serious, aren't you!"

Louisa nodded, a happy twinkle in her eye. "Pastor Dan and I have talked it over, and we'd like to put you through nurse's training at Colorado University."

Carrie's eyes grew wide. "But why. . .how?"

"We've never had children of our own, Carrie, as you

know." Louisa's voice grew soft. "For years we hoped and prayed, but God chose not to give us a child. All that time, though, we saved as much money as we could, hoping that someday. . ." She wiped a tear from her eye. "Anyway, you've been like a daughter to us these last few years, Carrie. We love you."

"I love you, too." Carrie hugged the pastor's wife tenderly. "You two have always been here for me."

"Here now, what are all these tears for?" Pastor Dan stood watching the two women in dismay.

"They're happy tears, Dan," his wife said. "I think Carrie has accepted our offer."

"Yes, I. . .how can I ever thank you two enough?" Carrie looked from one to the other.

"Well, get good grades for one thing," Pastor Dan teased. "Seriously, Carrie, we're glad to do it. And besides that, it's a kind of investment in our community. A lot of people around here depend on you."

Especially since Zach is gone, Carrie added silently. She nodded. "I do believe with my whole heart that this is where God has placed me. I promise to do my best."

seventeen

Zach had been wandering in places that were as dry as his soul. Wearily leading Pepper into a small grove of Russian olive trees, he mechanically unpacked his bedroll. Deftly building a fire, he sank down in front of it, having neither the strength nor the desire to fix himself a meal. As always, his thoughts drifted to Carrie, but he stubbornly pushed them away.

A slight noise startled him, and he quickly reached for his pistol. He held his breath, waiting. Soon a mother skunk and her four babies nosed out of the underbrush. Zach put his gun down with a sigh. *Getting a little skittish, aren't you?* he taunted himself. The long months in the saddle had brought no answers, only increased bitterness. Zach had lost track of time in his quest to find Frank and Clarence Yeakley. Instinctively, he knew that they held the key to the mystery.

Once I get my hands on them, I'll beat the truth out of them. He gritted his teeth. Never a man prone to violence, he had nevertheless let the cancer of bitterness and anger eat deeply into his soul. His own thoughts frightened him at times, but he had come too far now to turn back.

❧

It was always the same. Zach made his way from town to town, always searching. Being a traveling physician had its benefits. He could work until he had earned enough money for a few weeks, then head out onto the trail once more. Rarely now did thoughts of Carrie intrude on his mind. He had become like one consumed, vengeance his only goal. Doggedly he continued, certain that his quarry couldn't have disappeared into thin air.

One night found him slumped on a bar stool, weary to the

bone. "Most barns smell better than this dump," he muttered. Usually, he tried to avoid such places, but this town appeared to offer no other place where he could get a hot meal.

Gulping down the greasy, tasteless food, Zach revived somewhat. He watched with interest as the poker game going on across the room grew more animated, his pulse quickening as he saw the large amounts of cash exchanging hands. Watching intently now, he recalled the basics of the game learned in his years at medical school.

"Wanna join us, son?" A large man noted Zach's interest and waved him over.

A warning bell went off in Zach's head, but he ignored it. Settling gingerly into a vacant chair, he nodded to the group. "Name's Tanner."

*

Zach couldn't believe it. He counted the money again before stuffing it back into his boot. *If I'd have known how easy it is to win money, I wouldn't have wasted time working,* he thought ruefully. He remembered the look on the other men's faces after he had won three hands in a row. "I need to get going, gentlemen," he had said finally.

Coolly sweeping the cash off the table, he sauntered from the room. He had planned on leaving town that night, but couldn't resist staying one more day. If he could win big one more time, he'd have it made! The next evening found him at the poker table once again, his winnings from the night before spread out in front of him. He flashed a grin at the other men. "Can I buy you gentlemen a drink?"

Four drinks and three hands later Zach staggered out of the saloon, his pockets empty. "Guess it's me and you tonight, Pepper," he mumbled hazily. Stretching out beside the faithful horse, Zach sank into a deep sleep.

The violent nausea awoke him the next morning. He lay back on the hay, trembling. *This must be the reason I never drank before,* he groaned. Hours later, he stood, picking the straw off his clothes. Washing up quickly at the horse trough, he made his way back to the saloon. He was determined to win back what he had lost the night before.

The other men's amusement was clear as they greeted him. "Rough evening last night, eh, Tannner?" Conrad taunted.

Zach glared at him.

The other men burst into laughter. "I wouldn't look at Connie like that if I was you, Tanner," Al warned. "Come on, men. Let's get this game going."

Zach could feel Conrad's eyes boring into him all evening. Shrugging off the uneasy sensation, he played his best hand yet. "I'm calling it a night, men." Ignoring the dangerous look in Conrad's eye, Zach smiled as he slipped the cash off the table. "See you around."

⋄

Zach whistled happily as Pepper labored up the steep incline to yet another mountain town. He still couldn't believe his good fortune at the poker table. Why, with the amount of cash he had won, he wouldn't have to work for a couple of months. He smiled in satisfaction as he remembered the look on Conrad's face. Zach had half-expected to have some trouble on his hands, but a week had gone by with no sign of anything unusual.

"Guess Conrad and Al weren't as sore of losers as I'd thought," Zach told Pepper. "I thought sure they'd be after me to get their money back."

Pepper slowly trotted into the next filthy mining town. Zach looked around him in disgust. "I think we'll sleep under the stars tonight," he decided, urging the weary mare on.

A large copse of trees several miles out of town beckoned him. Zach quickly unsaddled Pepper, leaving her to graze on the sparse grass. Hurriedly gathering kindling before the daylight disappeared, he soon had a roaring blaze going. Evenings in the Rocky Mountains were chilly, even at this time of year. With a sigh, he eased himself to the ground. He sat watching pensively as the sun slipped behind the mountains. The night closed in on him, and still he didn't move.

The smell of the trees, the earth, had transported him to another time.

He had sat with Carrie amongst trees such as these, the sound of a rushing waterfall in the background. *"You have some wounds in your soul, Carrie. . .I know One who can heal them. . . ."* Zach's own words came back to him as if he had spoken them yesterday. *I know One who can heal. . .I know One. . .* The phrase rang over and over in his mind. Bitter tears began to fall, and Zach leapt to his feet in anguish. *But I don't know You anymore, God. I don't know You. . .I don't know. . . .*

eighteen

Sleep dropped over Zach like a heavy woolen cloak. Exhausted by the agony in his soul, he fell into a deep, dreamless sleep. Then suddenly he was wide awake. He reached for his pistol. A nameless fear crept over him as his body tensed, waiting.

What was it that had awakened him? Squinting, he tried to peer through the underbrush, but it was still too dark. He shivered, berating himself for letting the fire die down. He gripped his pistol tighter and edged in closer to the barely-glowing embers. Reaching for a stick of kindling, he froze. The sensation of being watched was so real it sent chills down his spine. He glanced around nervously. Nothing.

"Put down yer gun, Tanner."

The calm voice was so close to his ear, Zach dropped the pistol instantly. Whirling, he met the amused gaze of Conrad.

"Thought you pulled one over on us, didn't ya?" The big man smirked. "Come on out, boys. We done caught us a skunk."

Zach's heart sank as the five men surrounded him. *My God, what have I done?* He darted a glance at the men. They all had the same steely look in their eyes as their leader. Escape would be impossible.

"Tie 'im up, boys," Conrad instructed cheerfully. Striding over, he yanked Zach's boots off, gleefully extracting the wad of cash. "Had a feelin' you'd be an easy one," he gloated.

A feeling of dread washed over Zach. "What are you planning on doing with me?" he demanded. Maybe they would just leave him here, tied up, since they got their money back. . . .

His hopes were dashed with Conrad's next words.

"Well, we've got a little job for you to do, Mr. Tanner." The other men guffawed. "You wouldn't mind helping us out, now would ya?"

Zach glared at him.

"Aw, now look who's the sore loser," Conrad taunted. His smile suddenly gone, he whipped a small jug out of his saddlebag. "I was hopin' you would cooperate, but it don't appear yer goin' to." He soaked a small cloth with the contents of the jug.

Zach caught a faint whiff of the rag as Conrad corked the jug. *Ether! Dear God, what on earth are they going to do to me?*

He had no more time to think as the sweet-smelling cloth was slapped over his face.

❧

Zach moaned, the soft mud muffling the sound. Painfully opening his eyes, he was surprised to find himself alone. His eyes slid shut again as he tried to absorb this bit of information. The pain throbbing throughout his body seemed to be originating in his leg and he groaned as he forced his eyes open again.

He found himself staring at the muddy ground. From the warmth of the sun on his back, he knew it wouldn't be long before the mud was baked as hard as rock. He grimaced, wondering why he was concerned about mud baking when his whole body ached like a horse had walked on it. A horse! Where was Pepper?

Suddenly it all came back. He had held his breath the last time they tried to drug him. Pretended to be unconscious. . . tried to escape on Pepper. Conrad had caught him, and then. . . A wave of nausea swept over Zach as he recalled the bullet ripping through his thigh, the intense explosion of pain.

He should have just killed me, Zach thought. But no; what had Conrad said before he fired the shot? *Yer too valuable to me to kill ya, Tanner.*

Zach closed his eyes in exhaustion. *What did Conrad mean*

*by that? Besides, if he needed me for something, why am I
lying in this ditch with a bullet hole in my leg?* His thoughts
began to whirl as he slipped into unconsciousness once again.

๏

Night had fallen. Even in the cool evening air, Zach could tell
he was burning with fever. Still facedown, he didn't have the
strength to turn over.

". . .Call upon me in the day of trouble: I will deliver
thee. . ." The long-forgotten Scripture from Psalm 50 floated
into his mind. Slow tears trickled down his cheeks. "I can't,
God. I can't call upon You. I turned my back on You,
remember?" The dirt beneath his face became mud once
again as the hot tears continued to fall. "It's too late. I can't
call on You. . .I'm not worthy. . . ."

nineteen

"It's so nice to have you home from school for a while, Carrie."

"Thanks, Louisa. It's good to be here, if only for the holidays." Carrie paused. "How have things been going with the new doctor?"

"He's all right, I guess." Louisa wrinkled her nose. "I sure am glad he's only temporary, though. We're all looking forward to having our own Nurse Carrie back for good."

Carrie hid a smile. "Dr. Brown does seem a bit stuffy," she admitted, "but I'm sure he's doing a fine job."

Louisa rolled her eyes. "Just hurry up and finish. We miss you!"

Louisa's words rang in Carrie's ears for days. *I miss you, too. All of you,* she thought. Coming back home to Bailey after a semester at medical school had been bittersweet. How she had hoped and prayed that Zach would be waiting for her along with the rest of the town.

"I'm sorry, Carrie," Pastor Dan had said. "There's been no word of Zach that I know of."

She had tried to hide her intense disappointment, but when Louisa greeted her with a welcoming hug, the tears came thick and fast.

"I'm sorry, Louisa." Carrie stepped back, attempting to compose herself. "I had so hoped. . ."

"I know, child." Louisa's voice was compassionate. "But we mustn't give up hope."

Carrie put on her cheerful nurse's face, hiding her heavy heart. The days of her vacation slipped by. Before she knew it, Christmas was upon her.

Carrie had promised Louisa that she would be at the

114

Christmas Eve social, but regretted it the moment she stepped through the church door. Assailed by memories of Zach, she turned to go. Was it only a year ago that he had held her so tenderly? She hugged herself unconsciously. And how infinitely precious the gifts he had given her had become. Toby was her constant companion; the Bible her most prized possession. *Oh, Zach,* her heart cried. *Why did you have to leave?*

Stumbling blindly toward the door, she glanced up just in time to avoid a collision.

"Oh, Dr. Brown. I'm so sorry. I wasn't watching where I was going."

"Apparently not," he said stiffly. "You aren't leaving already?"

"Yes, I—"

"Oh, Carrie, there you are!" Annabelle Parker's high voice grated across Carrie's ears. "I was so hoping I'd have a chance to say hello to you while you were home."

Carrie nodded wearily. This evening was beginning to give her a headache. "Thank you, Annabelle. It's nice to see you, too. I was just—"

"And how are you and Philip getting along?"

"Philip?"

"Oh, I'm sorry." Annabelle widened her eyes. "I thought surely you and Dr. Brown were on a first-name basis."

Carrie glanced up at the frosty young doctor, then at Annabelle. What was she up to?

"Dr. Brown and I have only met briefly, Annabelle."

"Oh! I just thought. . . ." Annabelle let her words trail off. "You know, since you and Dr. Tanner were so close. . . ."

Carrie felt the blood rush to her face. "What does Zach have to do with this?"

Annabelle gave an injured gasp. "There's no need to get so upset, Carrie. I'm sure it's still a shock to you that Zach left so hastily just before the wedding."

Carrie's face was flaming. "Excuse me, Dr. Brown; Annabelle. I need to get back home."

"Why, Carrie, everyone is just getting here. You can't leave now." Annabelle's tone was pure innocence. "Besides, I never have told you how sorry I am that Zach got injured in the fight that night with Clarence Yeakley."

Yes, I'm sure you're very sorry, Annabelle, Carrie thought, inching out the door.

"It was partly my fault, you know."

Carrie froze. "What?"

"I feel very badly that it was because of me that Zach was out that night." Annabelle dabbed at her eyes. "Zach had been having supper at our house and was walking home when it happened, you know."

Carrie stepped out into the crisp December air. "Good night, Annabelle," she said firmly.

The tiny snowflakes stung her burning cheeks as she trudged home. *How could Annabelle have the nerve to imply. . .* Carrie stopped in her tracks. A memory of Annabelle on Zach's arm at the train station fluttered through her mind. Could Zach and Annabelle have been together while she was in Denver caring for May? She shook her head. It was too preposterous. *Zach couldn't really have just been performing when he looked at me so lovingly, could he?* She shook her head again.

"I know Zach loves me," she said out loud. *Loved you,* her mind corrected. *If he did love you, he would be back by now, wouldn't he?* Carrie sighed, gazing up at the brilliant stars. Zach had taught her the names of all the constellations last summer as they sat on the porch together. Her eyes automatically traced the lines of the Big Dipper, and she wondered if Zach could see the sky from wherever he was right now. *I know you're out there somewhere, Zach. Please come back to me. I need you.*

❧

As much as she tried to push Annabelle's insinuations from her mind, Carrie couldn't forget the questions that they were raising. Surely Annabelle was lying, but. . .

"Louisa, do you know where Zach was going that night

that Clarence Yeakley beat him up?"

Louisa glanced at Carrie curiously. "I assume he was going home to Mrs. Granger's, Carrie. Why?"

Carrie dropped her gaze. "I just wondered."

"I don't believe that for one instant, Carrie Winthrop. Now tell me what's bothering you."

Carrie kept her eyes averted. "I spoke with Annabelle Parker at the Christmas Eve social—"

"Oh, so that's it." Louisa's eye held a knowing look. "What kind of nonsense did she tell you this time?"

"She made my relationship with Zach sound so. . .so cheap." Carrie felt her face redden. "And she said that Zach had dinner at her house the night he was in that fight."

"And now you're wondering if Zach was carrying on with Annabelle behind your back."

Carrie nodded reluctantly. "Something like that."

"Well, let me tell you a thing or two, young lady!"

Carrie glanced up in surprise at the anger in Louisa's voice.

"That boy was no more seeing Annabelle than your daddy is Thaddeus Green. I know Zach's been gone a long time, but if you love him like you say you do, you'll not doubt him."

Carrie felt ashamed of herself. "It's just so hard, Louisa," she whispered. "Why doesn't he at least let me know he's all right?"

twenty

"Yup, looks like this is our man all right, Sheriff. Hope the scoundrel pulls through so we can give him what he deserves!"

The gruff voice grated across Zach's nerves. He groaned softly, claiming the attention of the two men who stood over him.

They stared down at him speculatively as he licked his lips. "Well, looks like the high and mighty James Vickers needs something," the sheriff taunted.

"Water," Zach croaked finally.

The sheriff crooked a finger at a young boy across the room. "Come here, young Andrew. I'm puttin' you in charge of this man."

The freckle-faced youth nodded seriously. "I'll git him all fixed up, Sheriff."

The lawman snorted. "Yeah, you do that. He's the most valuable prisoner I had in this jail in a long time."

A prisoner! Zach tried to grasp the implication of the sheriff's words, but his raging thirst blocked out all else. "Water!" he rasped again, reaching a beseeching hand to the boy.

❧

"There ya are, Mister," Andrew said, tucking a thin pillow under Zach's head.

Zach smiled wanly at his benefactor. The boy's hands had been surprisingly gentle as he tended to Zach's wound.

"Are ya hungry?"

Zach's eyes lit up. The cold water the boy had brought him earlier had been heavenly, but now his stomach felt terribly hollow.

He closed his eyes gratefully as the boy hurried away. Zach couldn't remember the last time he had slept on a bed.

Actually, this was a cot, but after what he had been through. . . His eyes flew open. *Where am I, anyway?* The plain gray walls and drab, curtainless window gave him no clues. He frowned. The room seemed remarkably bare except for the cot he was lying on. Struggling to sit up as he heard approaching footsteps, a flash of pain shot through his leg. He fell back to the pillow with a gasp.

The boy scurried to his side, hastily setting the tray of food on the floor. "Are ya all right, Mister?"

Zach nodded, his teeth clenched. Slowly the pain subsided and he took a deep breath.

"What am I doing here?" he whispered.

The youth's eyes widened. "Ya don't know?"

Zach shook his head.

His pint-sized guard glanced toward the door. "Here's yer supper."

Zach eyed the plate appreciatively. "My name's Zach Tanner. You can call me Zach."

The boy nodded, watching in silence as Zach satisfied his hunger. "Then how come they done said you was James Vickers?"

Zach shrugged and pushed the plate back. "You didn't answer my question."

"I'm not allowed to—"

"Please! I don't even know where I am!" Zach's voice was low, pleading. "The last thing I remember, I was lying in a muddy ditch, and now I'm here—wherever here is."

"Well. . .I guess it wouldn't hurt none to tell ya that yer in the county jail."

In the county jail? "But what county? Am I still in Colorado?"

"Colorado?" The boy looked blank. "This is Arizona. We just become a state," he added proudly.

"But. . .why?"

"Maybe he got hit in the head," Zach heard the boy mutter to himself. "Ya better rest some now, Mister—Zach. I'll be back in the morning." Almost as an afterthought, he stuck his head back in the door. "Yer cell is being guarded around the clock. Just thought I'd let ya know."

Wonderful. Zach sighed as he heard the key turn in the lock. *Looks like I'm here to stay, for a while at least.* He sighed again, suddenly too tired to think.

ò€

Even as the wound in Zach's leg healed, the wounds in his heart festered. Left alone for hours on end, he had nothing to do but think. He learned quickly that thoughts of Carrie were torturous, and instead turned his mind to the two men who had come to represent all his troubles. *If they hadn't done what they did, I would have never been in this filthy place,* he complained daily.

Hardening his heart to the quiet call of the One he used to know so well, Zach grew more miserable day by day. The sheriff had interrogated him more than once, frustrating them both to no end. Apparently the sheriff had found some evidence on Zach that led him to believe Zach was the notorious criminal, James Vickers. Zach insisted he was a doctor. No amount of protesting on his part could change the sheriff's mind until the day his wife's appendix almost burst. In desperation, the sheriff let Zach perform the arduous surgery. Thankfully, it was a success. The sheriff relented and telegraphed the medical school to confirm Zach's identity and year he had earned his medical degree.

But it still hadn't earned Zach his freedom. "Evidence is evidence, Tanner," the sheriff had said. Without a shred of proof of his innocence, Zach would have to remain in jail until the federal judge came to Arizona to conduct his trial. And no one knew when that would be.

ò€

Zach woke with a start, straining to hear. But to hear what? There it was again. . .ah, it was the key turning in the lock. *In the middle of the night?*

Someone must be sick, he thought bitterly. No one came to visit him unless that incompetent Dr. Bushnell was out of town. Then they lowered themselves to come to Zach. He snickered derisively. Who ever heard of a doctor that practiced out of a jail cell? The torchlight blinded him momentarily as the door flew open.

"Got a friend here for ya, Tanner. Hope ya don't mind sharing!"

Sharing what? Misery? He jumped to his feet as the sheriff shoved a man through the door and slammed it shut again.

Zach strained to see through the sudden darkness. "Who are you?" he called out.

A low moan answered him.

Moving cautiously lest it was a trick to lure him closer, Zach inched toward the sound of the labored breathing. "Who are you?" he whispered.

The man took a gasping breath. "Thirsty!" he whispered hoarsely.

Zach sighed. This man was no threat, at least not at the moment. Groping his way to the water bucket, he dipped a cup of water. *Of all the nights for there to be no moon,* he thought to himself.

The man drank greedily. "Bless you," he croaked.

Before Zach could question him, his new companion lapsed into a deep sleep where he lay. Zach sighed again. *I guess I'll have to wait until morning to meet my new "friend,"* he thought ruefully. *At least he's too weak to do anything to me while I sleep.*

He lay back down on the cot, pulling his blanket up over himself. A minute later, he got back up. Yanking the blanket off the cot with an exasperated sigh, he felt around until he found the man sleeping on the cold floor. Draping the blanket over the quiet figure, he stormed back to bed. *Now what did I do that for? I'm going to freeze all night.*

He flopped down, staring in the direction of the ceiling. The whole two years he had been here, there had never been another prisoner besides himself. There was the occasional ruffian or drunk locked up for a night or two, but they were always held in the small cell adjoining the sheriff's office. The room where Zach was imprisoned was apparently reserved for long-term residents. *Or particularly notorious ones,* he thought bitterly.

He glanced in the direction of his cell mate. *I wonder what horrible crime this man has done to be put in here with me?*

Could this be the man named Vickers? The thought startled him. *If it really is him, then I'm a free man.* He felt his palms grow sweaty; he felt the blood pounding in his head as the thought took hold.

"Please, God. Let it be him." Zach turned instinctively to the One he had scorned for so long, then stopped when he heard his own words. He had no right to call on God.

A night had never seemed so long. As soon as the first dim light of dawn stole into the cell, Zach hurried over to inspect his fellow prisoner, hoping he wasn't dead.

The man lay snoring softly, his arm flung over his face. Zach prodded him with his toe, then sprang back as the man jerked awake. His mouth dropped open as the man rolled to face him. "You!"

Clarence Yeakley looked equally shocked to see Zach. "Thought I hered the sheriff say the name Tanner last night. What are *you* doin' in here?"

"It's a long story, Yeakley." Zach spoke through clenched teeth. All the months he had hunted for this dog, and now he was locked in the same cell with him. He swallowed hard against the hatred that rose in his throat like bile. *Just bide your time, Tanner,* he instructed himself. *You'll have your chance.*

Clarence was watching him warily.

"Just stay away from me, Yeakley." Zach hated the way his voice shook.

"I'm not gonna try anything, if that's what ya mean, Zach." Clarence's voice was soft, almost placating.

Zach stared hard at him. "Just see that you don't."

twenty-one

Looking more closely at his fellow prisoner, Zach realized the man was seriously injured. "Apparently you couldn't try anything even if you wanted to, Yeakley," he scoffed.

The younger man grimaced. "Guess yer right, there, Doc. Think ya can fix me up?"

Zach laughed without mirth. This was impossible. *I hunt this man for months, then suddenly he's dumped in my lap.*

"I wouldn't help you if you were the last man on earth," he spat out.

Clarence's eyebrows shot up. "What's happened to ya, Tanner? Yer not the same—"

"No, I'm not the same, Yeakley. I'll never be the same, thanks to you and that miserable father of yours!"

"What?"

"Don't act so innocent, you dog! The two of you ruined my life, and now you're going to pay!" Without warning, he slammed his fist into Yeakley's nose. The pent-up anger came spewing forth as he landed blow after blow, not even noticing that the injured man wasn't fighting back. He drew his arm back for yet another blow.

"Jesus. . ."

The whispered name froze his arm in mid-air. Glancing down, he realized for the first time that Clarence was almost unconscious.

"What have I done?" Zach dropped to his knees beside his victim. The warm, metallic smell of blood assailed him, making him suddenly, violently ill. "Oh, God," he cried out loud. "Forgive me. . . ."

"What happened in here?" Sheriff Jergen strode into the small cell, then backed out, gagging.

"It's about time, Jergen." Zach glared at the lawman from his place beside the cot. "Get me some help in here fast unless you want to lose your prisoner."

He raised his eyes heavenward as Jergen left on the run. "Please, God, let him live. Let him live. . . ."

❧

Rebecca Frank straightened up wearily. "I think it's up to God now, Zach. Ain't much more either of us can do." The woman Sheriff Jergen had sent looked at Zach curiously. "You say the sheriff brought him in here in this condition?"

Zach dropped his gaze. "More or less," he murmured.

Rebecca's keen eyes swept the bloodstained floor. "I see," she said quietly. "How about I help you clean up this mess?"

❧

Zach lay on his blanket, too miserable to sleep. Each labored breath that Clarence Yeakley drew pounded the nails of guilt and remorse deeper into his heart. Longing to escape into the oblivion of sleep, he stuffed his fingers into his ears, drew a deep breath, and tried not to think.

Hours later, he woke with a start. What had awakened him? He strained to hear, but there were no unusual noises—no noises! He couldn't hear Yeakley breathing.

"Please God, no!"

He flew to the cot. Resting his head on the younger man's chest, Zach almost fainted in relief as he felt the steady rhythm of normal breathing. "Thank You, Jesus," he whispered.

A low chuckle startled him. "I thought I was the one who should be thankin' God," Clarence rasped.

Zach jumped up. "Just shut up, Yeakley," he ordered roughly. "Get some rest."

"Whatever ya say, Doc."

Zach lay back down, mystified. *Yeakley should hate me as much as I hate him, but he talked to me like I'm his friend.* He smiled grimly in the darkness. *Maybe I knocked him one too many times in the head after all.*

Dawn came much too early, spilling brilliant rays of sunshine into the dim cell. Zach groaned, burying his face in the blanket.

"When do ya get grub at this hotel?"

Zach sat up slowly, staring at his cell mate. "Are you always so cheerful after getting your head beat in?"

Clarence appeared to consider the question. "Naw," he said finally. "Only when it's a beating I deserved."

"What? Man, you are an idiot. You. . ." Zach finally noticed the twinkle in Clarence's eye. He felt the corners of his mouth twitch. "Did you deserve it?"

Clarence's smile disappeared. "Yeah, s'pose I did, after the way I treated you and Carrie." He paused when Zach flinched at Carrie's name. "Felt like a dog 'bout that fer a long time, and prayed that I'd have the chance to ask yer forgiveness."

Zach's mouth dropped open. "You're not the same," he finally managed.

"Could say the same 'bout you, Zach," the big man countered gently.

Zach gazed at the floor. "You got that one right," he mumbled. What exactly was going on here? This was not what he had planned to happen when he finally caught up with Clarence Yeakley.

"So—how 'bout it?"

"How about what?" Zach pulled his thoughts back to the present.

"Will ya fergive me?" Clarence's earnest blue gaze met Zach's wary brown gaze.

"Seems to me I ought to be the one asking that," Zach said at last.

Clarence shrugged. "Will ya?"

"I. . ." The simple word "yes" would bring instant release. Zach knew it, but something held him back. *How can I forgive just like that—just because he's asking me to? He ruined my life!*

Zach's heart constricted. *Someone has to pay for making me lose Carrie.* He turned his back so Clarence wouldn't see the sudden tears. "There is no forgiveness for you. You ruined my life."

"Ya talkin' 'bout Carrie?"

Zach swung around. "Of course I mean Carrie. How could you expect me to forgive you for perpetrating such a lie?"

Clarence blanched at the raw agony in Zach's eyes. "If ya'd let me explain, Doc—"

Zach snorted. "What's there to explain?"

"A terrible mistake what happened a long time ago. If ya'd jest hear me out. . ."

twenty-two

"Come on, Toby. It's getting late." Carrie waited patiently as the little dog followed her into the barn. Since that incident so long ago with Clarence Yeakley, Carrie always made sure Toby accompanied her as she did her chores. This night as she cared for Molasses, her heart turned wistfully to days gone by.

"I'll bet you miss Pepper as much as I miss Zach," she murmured to the mare. The scent of honeysuckle at the peak of bloom drifted lightly through the barn door, bringing with it the joyful memories of a summer that seemed to have been eons ago. *Could it only have been three years ago that I was sewing my wedding dress?* Sudden hot tears surprised her.

Molasses nickered softly, and Carrie automatically began to brush again with long, smooth strokes. Time had eased the sharpness of the pain, but had only increased the yearning. Only once in a while did she permit it to overwhelm her to the point of tears, but that scent of honeysuckle always reminded her of the night Zach had revealed his love for her.

Am I to live on memories alone, God? she cried. *I'm trying to trust You, but I miss him so much!*

Toby snuggled close to lick his mistress's tears. She buried her face in his soft fur and sobbed. *It's so hard to wait, God.* Eventually calming, she prayed the prayer that had become a source of strength to her in the past years. "I thank You, Lord, that You know the plans You have for Zach, plans to prosper and not to harm him, to give Zach hope and a future. And I also pray that Zach will not walk in the counsel of the wicked, or stand in the way of sinners, or sit in the seat of the mockers. But I pray that Zach's delight will be in the law of the Lord and that he will meditate on it day and night."

It helped so much to insert Zach's name into the Scriptures and pray for him aloud.

"I give Zach to You once again, Father," she prayed silently. "And I choose You, Jesus. I choose You over self-pity, over fear, over sadness and despair. I choose You."

❧

"Miss Winthrop, I need you to hold this child still!" Dr. Brown's voice matched his irritable personality.

Carrie struggled to hold her tongue. She was doing the best she could under the circumstances, and Dr. Brown knew that good and well.

"All right. I'm done." Dr. Brown walked away from the patient without another glance. "You can finish up for me, Miss Winthrop," he called over his shoulder.

Carrie pressed her lips into a tight line, refraining from throwing her bag at his back. *What kind of doctor would treat a patient like that? Especially one as sweet as little Jenna Galloway—*

"Miss Carrie?"

The little voice interrupted her silent tirade. "Yes, dear?"

"Am I going to be all better now?" Tears trembled in the six-year-old's eyes.

"Yes, Jenna, but not right away. You have a nasty break in that leg and you must be very still until it heals."

"Will it hurt very much?"

Carrie nodded reluctantly. "Yes, I'm afraid so, sweetheart. But not for too long." She took the little girl's hand. "Let's pray that Jesus makes it heal very fast."

Carrie took a deep breath as she stepped outside the Galloway house. Dr. Brown made it clear at every opportunity that he disliked this town and its people. *Why doesn't he just go practice somewhere else?* she griped silently. That was the original plan, anyway. He was only to fill in until Carrie got her nursing certificate, then he was to set up practice back in Boston.

It had been more than a year since Carrie had come back for

good, and he was still here. *Why doesn't he just go away?* she asked herself irritably as she plodded home. Suddenly feeling weary at the prospect of going home to her lonely house, she veered left and headed for Pastor Dan and Louisa's. They were always glad to share good conversation and a cup of hot lemon balm tea.

Passing the Parkers' house as she hurried along, she couldn't help noticing the pair on the front porch. Annabelle was giggling softly, gazing up into the eyes of Dr. Brown. Carrie stopped in her tracks, squinting through the dusk. Surely that wasn't Dr. Brown. He was actually smiling!

Realizing that she was staring, Carrie lowered her gaze and resumed her trek to Louisa's. *Well, at least the mystery has been solved.* She chuckled. No wonder the obnoxious Dr. Brown was still in Bailey. Annabelle had her claws in him, no doubt promising him a large dowry if he would marry her.

She frowned at her catty thoughts and sent up a quick prayer for forgiveness. *God, I need Your grace to deal with that woman,* she prayed, trying to be sincere.

From then on, Carrie found herself almost pitying the miserable Dr. Brown. *If he thinks he's unhappy now, wait until he has to live with Annabelle Parker day in and day out,* she told herself. The mere thought of it made her grimace.

❧

Walking home from church a few days later, a sudden gust of wind sent her hat flying, reminding her that autumn wasn't far away. She chased her wayward hat until it finally came to a stop against the Fiskers' barn. Reaching for it, she noticed something lying a few feet away. Curious, she walked over and picked it up. It appeared to be a page from a letter, and Carrie felt her cheeks redden as her eyes caught the words at the bottom of the page. "All my love, Philip." Apparently this letter was not meant for her eyes. It must be Annabelle's. She debated with herself about leaving it where she had found it, but decided the wind would blow it away. Even though she and Annabelle were not exactly on the best of terms, Carrie couldn't justify throwing it away. *I'll give it to her the next time I see her,* she decided, pocketing the page.

The next morning as Carrie pulled on her coat, she heard the crinkle of paper. Frowning, she put her hand in her pocket. *Oh, the letter.* She had forgotten all about it. *I'd better put it with my Bible so I don't forget to take it to church Sunday.* Thrusting it between the pages of her Bible, she hurried over to Louisa's.

Pastor Dan met her as she let herself in. "Carrie! I was just headed toward your house—"

"What's happened?"

Pastor Dan seemed hesitant, as if he didn't want to tell her. "There's been word of a bad accident."

"Where?" Carrie headed toward the door, then glanced back at her friend when he didn't reply.

"A man was mauled by a bear."

"A man? Who?" Carrie couldn't understand Dan's apparent reluctance. "I can't help him if I don't know who or where he is!"

The elderly minister sighed heavily. "I don't think you know him, Carrie. He moved out of town years ago. In fact, I didn't even know he was still in these parts."

Carrie jammed her hat on and grasped the doorknob. "Where can I find him?"

"Henry will have to take you. He's the one who found the old man." Dan frowned. "It'll be a hard ride, Carrie. The cabin is up in the high country."

She pictured the hulking figure of Henry Young. She had always secretly thought that the huge trapper looked like a bear, but he had one of the softest hearts of anyone she knew. "I'll be fine. Tell Henry I'll meet him in front of Daley's in ten minutes."

Carrie was halfway down the street when Dan caught up with her, his breath coming in short gasps. "Be careful, Carrie." His eyes pleaded with her. "Don't do anything foolish."

What was he so upset about? She patted his arm gently.

"Don't worry. I'll be fine."

❧

Carrie settled comfortably into Molasses' saddle. It had been too long since the two of them rode into an adventure.

"How did you find the man?" she called to the scout riding ahead of her.

"Well, I been out huntin' fer a week or so, and. . ."

Between the noise of the horses' hooves and Henry's confusing, long-winded story, Carrie could only surmise the injured man had been incredibly lucky that anyone had found him at all.

Two hours had passed, and Carrie no longer felt adventurous. She couldn't ride the way she used to, she admitted to herself. She rubbed her lower back ruefully, recalling the five- and six-hour rides she and Zach had often taken. What fun they had had on those rides. *Ah, Zach. . .* She shook her head. It would do no good to dwell on such thoughts.

"Henry!" She shouted over the steady thump of the horses' hooves. "Can we take a little break?"

Henry threw her a grin over his shoulder. "Yup. Let's stop over by the river."

Carrie dismounted stiffly. Ambling down to the rushing flow, she dipped a handful of icy water.

"Won't be much longer before the first snowstorm, I reckon," Henry commented, wiping his mouth on his sleeve. "That water's as cold as it gets 'fore it turns to ice."

"You can say that again!" Carrie's teeth ached from just one sip. She took a deep breath of the pine-scented air, stretching her arms over her head to relieve some of the tension in her neck. "Are we almost there?"

Henry nodded. "Jest about half an hour more, I reckon. Are you ready?"

"In a minute." Carrie stared into the rushing water for a long minute. "Do you know this man that I'm going to treat?"

Henry's shaggy eyebrows shot up. "Ever'body knows who Frank Yeakley—"

"Yeakley?" Carrie's heart constricted.

"Is something wrong, Miss Carrie?"

"No. . .I—we're going to Frank Yeakley's cabin? He's the one that's injured?"

Henry gave her a strange look. "Didn't Pastor Dan tell ya nuthin'?"

"All he told me was that you had found a man that had been mauled by a bear, and that my assistance was needed."

"Oh. But. . .if you don't know Frank, then how is it he asked for ya by name?"

Carrie's heart began a slow, pounding thump that resounded in her ears. "I don't know, Henry." *And maybe I don't want to know,* she thought.

Her mind whirling, she remounted Molasses. "Let's go, Henry. I'm ready."

They followed the river for fifteen more minutes or so, then Henry motioned for her and Molasses to follow him into the icy water. The horses forded the river easily, then patiently resumed plodding up the trail. Carrie grimaced as her tailbone was subjected to more punishment. Could it be possible that she would find out the truth about her father? *If Frank Yeakley was indeed the man Zach was hunting for, then surely. . .* She tensed as a new thought occurred to her.

What if Zach had located Yeakley and found out the truth months ago, and had decided not to return to her? *Surely it was possible. . . . No. Zach was a man of his word.* Even if he didn't love her anymore, he would have come back to tell her what he'd found out.

Carrie gazed far ahead at the snowcapped peaks that surrounded her. "I will lift mine eyes unto the hills, from whence cometh my help." *My help. . .* The Scripture from Psalm 121 rose to her lips as she considered what lay ahead of her. She smiled slightly. "You are my true Father, God," she whispered. "No matter if I never find out the truth about my earthly father, I'll always be Your daughter."

Feeling comforted, she rode on in silence until Henry

abruptly reined in. "This is it, Miss Carrie." He gestured toward a dilapidated cabin. "Hope we're not too late."

Carrie nodded grimly. Clambering from the saddle, she swung her bag down and stood still for a brief moment. *Go before me, please, Father,* she breathed.

The two rescuers gagged at the stench that greeted them as Henry kicked the door open. Carrie stood still, letting her eyes adjust to the darkness. Following the sound of raspy breathing, she discovered an elderly man lying on a cot against the far wall.

"Quick! Light a lamp, Henry," she called. *At least he was still alive. . . .*

Henry banged around, searching for a lantern. When the light finally blazed, Carrie sucked in her breath sharply.

The man lying in front of her barely resembled a human being. Claw marks raked into Yeakley's face and arms were angry, festering sores. Clumsily tied, blood-soaked bandages covered his torso and legs.

Henry frowned. "I bandaged 'im up best I could when I found 'im, Carrie." He glanced at the dying man. "I weren't goin' ta leave 'im. I knew he prob'ly weren't goin' ta make it, but he begged me to go fetch ya."

Carrie straightened her shoulders, mentally loosening herself from the grip of the horrifying scene. "We need to make him as comfortable as possible, Henry. He doesn't have long."

At the sound of her voice, the man's eyes flew open. "You came."

Carrie nodded. "Yes, I'm the nurse. Now just try to rest. Henry and I will—"

"You're my daughter."

Carrie started. "What did you say?"

Yeakley coughed violently, his face contorting with pain. "You. . .are. . .my. . .daughter."

Henry touched Carrie's arm gently. "He's out'n 'is head. He don't know what he's sayin'."

Carrie ignored Henry's words. Falling to her knees in front of the cot, she grasped Yeakley's cold hand. "Are you telling me the truth? Are you my father?"

"Carrie—"

"Hush, Henry." Carrie turned her gaze back to Yeakley. Dismayed to find that his eyes had closed, she touched his forehead with a gentle hand. "Can you hear me, Frank?"

She almost missed the slight nod.

"What was my mother's name?"

"Shar. . .Sharayah." The name came out in a whispered sigh.

Carrie sat back on her heels. "Frank Yeakley really is my father, Henry," she whispered.

"Are ya sure? Carrie, the man's half dead. Surely ya ain't gonna believe—"

"He is my father, Henry. It's a long story." It suddenly all made sense. She stood up. "We need to tend to these wounds."

Yeakley's eyes fluttered open. "No use," he rasped. "Gonna die."

Carrie dropped down onto the earthen floor again. "Are you ready to die, Frank? Do you know God?"

"Don't. . .want. . .me."

Carrie's eyes filled with tears. "Yes, yes, He does want you. God wants everyone to know Him. He'll forgive you of everything you ever did if you just ask Him to."

"Lied about. . .Thad. . .had him. . .killed."

"I know, Frank." Carrie was unaware of the tears flowing down her cheeks. "But that doesn't matter now. All that matters is that you ask God to forgive you."

Frank's eyes slipped closed. Carrie threw her bag open and grabbed her Bible. "It says right here in Second Peter 3:9 that the Lord is 'longsuffering to usward, not willing that any should perish, but that all should come to repentance.' That means you, too, Frank." She laid her hand on his arm. "Will you do it? He's waiting for you to come to Him."

Frank's eyes remained closed, but slow tears squeezed out

and began to trickle down his face.

Carrie prayed silently, watching this stranger that was her father. When a peaceful smile stole over his countenance, her heart leapt.

"Tell. . .Clarence."

Carrie blanched. She never wanted to see Clarence Yeakley again, much less—

"Tell Clarence," Frank said with more force. "He needs. . . God. . .too."

Carrie grasped his hand. "I will, I promise." *God, help me.*

The whispered words seemed to satisfy him, and he fell into a deep, coma-like sleep.

Carrie sat beside his cot, her Bible on her lap. She read chapter after chapter aloud, sometimes stopping to pray. After what seemed hours, Frank suddenly opened his eyes. "I love you, Carrie."

His clear statement startled her. "I. . .love you, too. . .Papa."

He smiled and let his head fall back with a sigh.

Carrie jumped up and grasped his hand, but even before she touched him she knew he was gone. Laying his hand gently back down, she finally gave in to the storm of tears that had been gathering all afternoon.

"Thank You, God!" She sobbed into Henry's sturdy shoulder for long minutes before finally pulling away. "I'm so glad we made it in time."

Henry nodded, an awed look on his face. "Me, too, Miss Carrie. Me, too."

twenty-three

Zach stared hard at the man he had hated for so long. Could he really expect Clarence Yeakley to tell the truth? Zach sighed heavily. "All right. Tell me your story."

Clarence sat up straighter. "It's not a purty tale, Zach. But I promise ya—it's the truth."

Zach allowed a slight smile to come to his lips. "I'll decide that on my own, Yeakley."

Clarence grinned in response, then sobered. "Never thought I'd get a chance to tell ya this. God knows I've wanted to. . . ." He closed his eyes briefly, then gazed at Zach. "I know what ya been thinkin' all this time, but Carrie ain't *your* sister; she's *my* sister."

"What?" Zach jumped to his feet, nearly knocking Clarence to the floor.

Clarence grinned. "She don't have a drop of yer pa's blood runnin' through her veins."

"Are you sure?" Zach's voice was a hoarse whisper.

"Yep." Clarence's smile dropped then. "I took a shine to her once, Zach. I couldn't understand why Pa wouldn't let me court her." He shook his head. "I pestered 'im about it until he finally broke down and confessed."

"Confessed what?"

"Pa had been to see Sharayah several times when he found out she was pregnant—with Carrie. My ma never did find out the truth," he added sadly. "Pa made me swear I would never tell no one. But considerin' what I done, I reckon I owed ya th—"

Zach's thoughts were reeling. "Then what about my father? Who killed him?"

"*That* I don't know," Clarence admitted. "I reckon my pa

and the sheriff was in on it, but neither o' them done it."
Clarence gazed at Zach apologetically. "I heard they paid a
drifter ten dollars to do it."

Ten dollars! What was this world coming to when a man's
life was worth only ten dollars? Zach closed his eyes. "I think
I've heard all I need to, Yeakley."

Clarence painfully hoisted himself back up onto the cot. He
lay down with a sigh, turning his back to the aching man.

Zach realized that Clarence was attempting to give him
some privacy and he appreciated the gesture, but his soul was
too numb. He couldn't cry; he couldn't rave. All he could do
was stare at the wall. *All this wasted time. . .I forsook the
woman I love, the profession I love, even the God I love to
find the truth. And all I have to show for it is two years in a
stinking jail cell and an enemy that treats me like a friend.*

Sleep eluded him for nights on end. His conscience would
not let him rest. Finally he broke the self-imposed silence.
"You're not the same Clarence Yeakley I knew in Bailey."

Clarence glanced up, startled at the first words Zach had
spoken in a week. Quickly masking his surprise, he responded
cheerfully. "Thought ya'd never notice."

Zach grunted. "Well?"

Clarence gave him a steady, almost pitying look. "Don't ya
know, Zach? I let God change my life. I'm not the same
Clarence, like ya said."

Zach raised an eyebrow. "What are you doing in here, anyway? Been stealing horses again?"

Clarence winced at the implication. "I wish it was jest
that," he said sadly. "My God, how I wish!"

Zach stared as the tears poured down Clarence's cheeks.
This was no act.

"Does the name Vickers mean anything to ya, Zach?"

He felt the hairs on the back of his neck prickle. Was this a
trap? Had Sheriff Jergen planted Clarence to try to get information out of him? Well, it wasn't going to work. He shook his
head slowly. "Can't say I know anyone named Vickers. Why?"

Clarence drew a deep breath. "James Vickers is the head honcho of a gang of thieves."

Zach raised his eyebrows. This was interesting. Perhaps he was finally going to find out what he was being accused of.

"Anyway, after I left Bailey, I lived with my pa fer a while, then struck out on my own and fell in with Vickers' group. We was real good, and I was livin' high on the hog." Clarence shook his head. "I didn't have no qualms 'bout taken jewels from rich folks, but Vickers come up with a new plan. Kidnapping. We'd ask fer a ransom, or jest sell the little ones somewheres."

Zach sucked in his breath. No wonder the entire town hated him! Kidnappers were among the worst kind of criminals as far as most people were concerned.

Tears welled up in Clarence's eyes once more. "I couldn't do it, Doc." He swiped at his eyes. "They done took a girl. . . and I ain't been a very nice person all my life, but I jest couldn't stand the fear in the little mite's eyes." He closed his eyes in pain. "I was s'pose to be guardin' her, but I snuck 'er back home. Told Vickers she got away on her own."

Silence reigned for several long minutes. Zach cleared his throat. "Then what happened?"

"Got caught durin' a jewelry theft. Been in jail fer a year and a half." Clarence gave a half-smile. "Then I was brung here."

Zach cleared his throat, a tiny flame of hope flickering in his soul. "Do you know where Vickers is?"

"Last I heard they was headed to Colorado." Clarence shrugged. "The law will catch up to him one day."

"They think I'm him."

"What?"

"Sheriff Jergen thinks I'm James Vickers."

Clarence stared at Zach. "That's hogwash. Why would he think—"

"I don't know." Zach felt suddenly weary. "I, too, fell in with a bad crowd. I ended up in a ditch with a bullet in my leg. The next time I came to, I was in this cell. I've tried to explain, but. . ."

Zach's words trailed off at the look on Clarence's face. "What's wrong?"

"You—I can't believe it." Clarence looked at Zach like he'd never seen him before. "Were ya in with Conrad?"

Zach started. "Yes, but how—"

"Bad news, Conrad is. Worked with him a coupla times. 'Bout two years ago, things were gettin' a little hot fer us here in Arizona. We run into Conrad's gang one night. They was gripin' 'bout a double-crosser." Clarence drew a deep breath. "Please tell me that wasn't you."

The crickets tuning up in the long prairie grasses outside the cell walls were the only noise for a long moment.

Finally Zach shrugged.

Clarence groaned, shaking his head. "I can't believe it. We worked out a deal fer the poor feller. They brung him—you—to Arizona in exchange fer a sum of money. We took it from there."

Zach sat up straight. "Then your men planted that pocketwatch on me! But why?"

"No one 'round here knows what James Vickers looks like. We figgered if they found someone with evidence on 'im that pointed to Vickers, maybe they'd think it was him and lay off our trails. Guess it worked," he added wryly.

The tiny flicker of hope in Zach's heart was fast becoming a fire. "Would you be willing to explain to Jergen what you just explained to me?"

Clarence shrugged. "I don't see—"

The cell door crashed open. Sheriff Jergen strode into the cell, his face ashen. "They're pressing me for a trial, Tanner."

Zach rose to his feet. "What are you saying, Jergen?"

"Either I start a trial today, or. . ."

Zach's mind filled in the unspoken words. Just the thought of the lynching rope made beads of sweat pop out on his forehead. Raucous shouts filled the air outside the cell, and Zach slumped down on the cot in defeat. *Why now, God? Just when I found out the truth.*

"I'm sorry, Tanner. You know I've held off as long as I could, hoping to find the real Vickers, but I can't play games with them much longer. They know the evidence was found on you. They say they've waited two years and they're not waiting any longer." He ran a finger around the inside of his collar, grimacing as he tried to loosen it. "Look, Tanner. I know you're not guilty, but I don't have a choice!"

Zach heard the desperation in Jergen's voice and knew the lawman was right. The angry mob was going to have someone's head, and if it wasn't Zach's, it would be the sheriff's.

Zach glanced up, his eyes dull. "Let's get it over with, then."

Jergen appeared relieved. "I'm sorry, Tanner. At least with a trial, maybe you have a fighting chance."

Zach shrugged. The numbing emptiness in his soul seemed to take over his mind as he watched the sheriff pull out a short length of rope.

"I've got to bind your hands. I'm sorry." The sheriff looked grim.

"Wait!"

Zach jumped. He had forgotten that Clarence was even in the cell.

"I'll go."

"What?" Zach stared at Clarence. What kind of terrible joke was he playing?

Jergen dropped the rope, his mouth agape. "What did you say?"

"I said I'll take his place."

"Why?"

" 'Cause he's a good man, and he's innocent. And I can prove it."

The sheriff walked over to Clarence, looking him full in the face. "Do you know what you're saying, son?" He nodded to the window. "Those men out there aren't playing games. They want blood."

"I know that."

The lawman looked from Clarence to Zach, then back to Clarence. "You two sure became good buddies in the short time you've been in here together." His voice was doubtful.

Zach lifted the corners of his lips in the imitation of a smile. "We go back a long way."

Jergen raised his eyebrows, then looked back at Clarence. "You say Tanner is innocent, to which I agree. But you're not Vickers, either." He slammed his fist against the wall with a curse. "I hate that I'm being forced into this."

"How long before the trial is to begin?" Clarence's voice was calm.

The lawman rubbed his hand over his eyes wearily, his anger spent. "I don't know." Stepping over to the tiny window, he gazed outside for several silent minutes. "I'm going to come back to this cell in one hour. You two clowns decide which one of you wants to die." Shaking his head, he slipped out the door amid boos and hisses from the unruly mob. "All right, quiet down out here. The trial starts in an hour."

Silence reigned in the cell as the two prisoners stared at each other.

"Why are you doing this, Yeakley?"

Clarence smiled, but his eyes remained intense. "Jesus gave His life fer me and I was a stinkin' thief, Zach. He gave me freedom and a new life." Tears welled up in the big man's eyes. "I'd like to do that for ya."

"But. . .why? All I've done is hate you. I didn't tell you this before, but I had been searching for you for months before I ended up in here." Zach's voice dropped to a whisper. "I was going to get the truth out of you, then kill you." He glanced up in time to see compassion flood Clarence's eyes.

"That don't matter now, Zach. I've forgiven ya, and God will, too, if ya ask Him to."

Zach's gaze slid back down to the floor. "I'm no use to God anymore. He doesn't need a traitor."

"Doc Tanner."

Zach's head jerked up, and Clarence moved over to stand in front of him. "God's Word says in First John 1:9 that 'If we confess our sins, he is faithful and just to forgive us our sins, and to cleanse us from all unrighteousness.' And God don't lie."

Zach's heart burned within him, as the long-forgotten power of God's Word pierced his heart.

"And if God don't lie, then He'll fergive ya. I know it, 'cause that's what done happened to me."

"I don't know if I can accept that."

Clarence grinned, this time in earnest. "Ya will."

Zach studied the man before him, this foe-turned-friend. "I don't know what to say to you."

"Jest promise me one thing, Doc."

Zach nodded.

"Find my pa and tell him about Jesus."

Zach blanched. "I can't do that—who am I to tell someone else about God?" His words ended on a cry of anguish. He leaned against the wall, the rough coolness biting into his forehead. "God! I don't even know You any more!" Silent sobs wracked his body. He vaguely felt a strong hand clamped on his shoulder. Gradually quieting, he heard Clarence's quiet words of intercession.

He took a deep breath. "I promise you I'll do my best, Clarence."

His friend nodded. "I know I can trust ya, Zach. Ya got a good heart." Suddenly his eyes misted. "Tell Pa I want to meet him in heaven."

Zach swallowed against the lump in his throat. "Where can I find him?"

"He's been livin' in the high country." Clarence described the location briefly.

Zach couldn't believe his ears. "All those months I searched for the two of you, and he was there all that time. I don't believe it."

"God had plans fer ya other than becoming a murderer, Doc."

Zach grimaced.

"Besides, I hear tell there's a purty little nurse still waitin' fer ya to come home." Clarence chuckled at the look on Zach's face. "Go on home where ya belong, Doc. You'll be welcomed with open arms."

Zach shook his head. "Don't think so, Clarence. But I will go and find your father if it's the last thing I do."

But as much as he tried to deny it, his heart had leapt at the thought of Carrie. *Surely she's forgotten me by now. . .*

"One more thing, Zach. Tell my sister how sorry I am. . . ."

The room was silent again as each man looked deep within his soul; one contemplating the freedom of death, the other the freedom of life.

Long minutes later, the door swung open. The sheriff stepped into the cell, his face a mask. "It's time, gentlemen."

twenty-four

Zach slipped out of town a free man soon after the sheriff had led Clarence away. The two men had said all that needed to be said, and Zach had no desire to watch his newfound friend pay the ultimate price. Still, something held him, and he found himself waiting in the deep shadows of the trees on the edge of town. Waiting. . .waiting. . .

Dusk had deepened to twilight before he crept out of his hiding spot. Making his way to a precipice, he cautiously peered over the edge. His stomach lurched at the sight of the now-empty noose, swaying gently in the breeze. *It should have been me. . . .*

❧

Lying on his back, Zach breathed deeply of the pine-scented air as he gazed toward the night sky. He spotted the Sirius, the brightest star in all the heavens. Then to the north was Aldebaran. *Somewhere, Carrie lived under these same stars.* He smiled at the thought.

It felt so good to be free! Though he had enjoyed the beauty of the world around him all his life, nothing compared to sleeping under the stars after two years in a gray cell.

His mind replayed the events of the past month. As always, it seemed too fantastic to be true. Why would someone be willing to die for him? He had puzzled over this as he trudged over mile after endless mile of Arizona's red clay dirt.

As far as he could figure, Clarence must have done a whole lot of rotten things in his life. Had he been trying to make it up to God?

Zach sighed again, unable to figure it out. Pulling his hat over his eyes, he attempted to sleep. Tomorrow was another day, another few miles closer to home.

Home? Somehow the word brought images of Carrie, her eyes laughing, her mouth gentle as it pressed against his. More and more he was allowing himself the luxury of believing that she was still waiting for him. *Just for tonight,* he promised himself. *Just let me dream of her tonight, and then I'll forget all about her.*

છ

All through the long, scorching summer, Zach doggedly worked his way back toward Colorado. Bone weary, he would hire on at a ranch for a couple of weeks to earn enough money to get himself another hundred miles or so. As the hay-scented summer days turned into autumn, Zach made it to within a few days of Bailey. The familiar sights and smells quickened his pulse, making him feel truly alive for the first time in months.

And would she be there? Was there any way possible that she would still be waiting for him—maybe even still love him—after all this time? Her smiling face floated across his mind's eye, and he could almost smell the scent of her skin. "God, if You really still care—" The beginning of the prayer froze on his lips as he realized what he was doing. Clapping his hat on his head, he stormed across the open prairie, determined to escape his own tormenting thoughts.

Periodically checking the crude map Clarence had scribbled out for him, Zach judged he was a couple days' travel away from Frank Yeakley's cabin. His turmoil grew as he neared his destination. Duty and responsibility warred against the overwhelming desire to make a run for Bailey and Carrie. The only thing that stopped him was that she would *know*. She would be able to see the blackness of his soul in an instant.

Finally, he decided to slip into town for some much-needed supplies. He waited until dusk, then feeling like a criminal, he stole into the back entrance of Daley's Store. Quickly scanning the small establishment, he breathed a sigh of relief. Mr. Daley was the only one in sight, and he had his back turned.

Zach cleared his throat quietly, then louder. Mr. Daley turned, his mouth dropping open as he saw Zach.

"Dr. Tanner! It's so good to see you! I didn't even hear you come in."

Zach was relieved at the genuine warmth in the store-keeper's voice. He grinned at the older man. "Surprised you recognized me with this fuzz on my face." He indicated his shaggy beard. "It's good to see you again, Hank."

"Where ya been, son? You look terrible." The frank question was typical of Hank, but it rubbed the wound anyway.

"It's a very long story, Hank. I'm sure you'll hear the sordid details later, but. . ." Zach let his words trail off as he fiddled with a box of tenpenny nails that sat on the counter. Feeling his face color, he glanced up a Hank. "Could you just keep this under your hat for a few days, Hank? There are a couple of things I need to take care of before I come ho— before I come back, that is."

Hank's keen blue gaze probed Zach's face. "I'll keep my mouth shut. You in some sort of trouble, son?"

"No, I just—" Zach detected a movement out of the corner of his eye. Crouching down, he hid himself only seconds before a tall, serious-looking man entered the store. Zach felt incredibly foolish, but he was determined to make things right before he came back for good. Besides, he wanted to get to Carrie before anyone else told her he was in town. *I at least owe her that much.* He smirked at his thoughts. *You owe her a lot more than that, buddy, after what you did.*

He shifted uncomfortably, waiting for Hank's customer to leave. From his unusual vantage point, he studied the man idly, taking in the dull eyes and unpleasant attitude. *Bet he's a real joy to be around.* Zach almost laughed at the man's dour expression.

Finally the man turned to go. "Thanks for stopping in, Doctor Brown," Hank called.

Doctor Brown? Zach restrained himself from popping up out of his hiding place. Staring at the man's broad back, Zach felt searing stabs of jealously pierce his heart.

Hank peered down at Zach, amusement dancing in his eyes. "Comfortable?"

Zach glared at him. "Who was that?"

"Doc Brown." Hank made a face. "He was only supposed to be here temporarily to help out, you know, after. . .uh. . ." He looked at Zach apologetically. "Unfortunately, it looks like we're stuck with him for a while at least."

Zach didn't want to hear any more. Grabbing a razor, a cake of soap, and a few tins of food, he paid Hank and turned to go.

"Don't stay away so long this time, son."

Zach nodded without turning around. Sick at heart, he stumbled through the deepening twilight. *Surely you didn't think you could just waltz in here and take up where you left off?* his mind taunted him. *Life goes on. Bailey has a new doctor; Carrie probably has a husband. There's nothing left for you here.*

He stuck to the outskirts of the town, ducking behind a tree once or twice to avoid being seen. Gradually he stilled his racing thoughts. *I can't start up to the high country tonight. I'd get hopelessly lost.* More tired than he'd ever been in his life, he suddenly realized where his footsteps had taken him.

The light streaming from Carrie's parlor window beckoned him with a familiar, warm glow. His heart began to pound as he saw her rise from the chair by the fireplace, a book in her hand. It took every ounce of will that he still possessed not to run to her. His lips tingled with the remembrance of their last kiss; his arms ached to hold her. *Oh, God, please help me.*

Moistening his lips, he tore himself away, forcing his feet to move. He got as far as the barn before his strength gave way. Silently unlatching the barn door, he slipped inside. The warm, horsey smell enveloped him, bringing with it a measure of comfort.

Molasses shied as he came near. "Don't you remember me, old girl?" His movements were slow as he put out his hand,

and the horse pricked her ears forward in interest. She snuf-
fled tentatively at his hand, then whinnied in joy. Zach smiled
as he gave her a pat. "At least you're glad to see me," he murmured. Removing his hat, he wearily spread his blanket in the
clean stall next to Molasses, trying not to think about Pepper.

I just need to close my eyes for a few minutes. . . .

twenty-five

Carrie hummed softly as she headed out to do the morning chores. Autumn was such a beautiful time of year, even if it meant the snow would be here soon.

"Come on, Toby!" She looked for the little dog, then laughed as he came galloping toward her. "You've been in the creek again, haven't you, you little rascal!"

Toby shook joyously, mud and water flying everywhere.

Carrie wrinkled her nose. "Phew! You'd better stay out of the house until you dry."

Toby gave her hand a short lick, then pranced ahead of her toward the barn. Abruptly, he stopped, the fur on his neck standing on end. A low growl rumbled in his throat.

Carrie stopped, alarmed. "What is it, boy?" she whispered. Her grip tightened on the heavy stick she always carried at chore time. Toby had acted this way on occasion when a skunk or a stray dog had gotten into the barn. "It's probably just an animal," she said out loud. Hearing her own voice steadied her thoughts, and she reached for the door. Breathing a prayer for safety, she kicked the door open, her stick ready. Nothing happened.

Toby stopped growling once the door was open, and now he trotted in, nose to the ground. Several seconds went by as Carrie waited outside. Suddenly, short, joyful barks sounded from somewhere inside. Carrie let out her breath, rolling her eyes. "Must be that female dog again," she muttered. *No wonder he's so happy.* She peeked into the empty stall where Toby was still barking. There was nothing there. Puzzled, she watched the little dog run around in frantic circles, sniffing the floor every few feet.

Finally he tired and sat under the small window. He looked

at Carrie and barked expectantly.

She had to laugh. "What are you trying to tell me, boy? Did your lady love disappear?"

She turned to her chores with a smile. As she swept, she tried to plan her day. First she had to go check on the little Tomkins boy who was getting over the measles. *Then I'd better go see Lucille,* she decided. Pregnant with her seventh child and worn to a frazzle, Lucille was Carrie's most worrisome patient. Carrie sighed. Just thinking about talking to Lucille made her weary. *And I really ought to check at the post office again. Perhaps Henry left me a message by now. I think a visit with Louisa would do me good.*

"Come on, boy." Carrie whistled for Toby, who was still sitting in the empty stall. He came reluctantly, and as she stooped down to pat his head, something caught her eye. Bending down, she picked up a large button off the floor.

Turning it over and over in her hand, she stared at it. "This seems to have come off of someone's coat—a man's coat," she said out loud. "Toby, is this what you were trying to tell me?" Sudden fear gripped her. She ran to the window in the the empty stall. Sure enough, large footprints marred the soft mud outside.

She sank down to the floor, an image of Clarence Yeakley's leering face filling her mind. What if he came back? *God hath not given us the spirit of fear; but of power, and of love, and of a sound mind. . .* The bit of Scripture flowed into her mind, bringing a measure of peace. *Thank You, Father.* Rising on shaky legs, she locked the barn door behind her.

❧

Pastor Dan and Louisa exchanged glances as Carrie related the incident.

"Perhaps you shouldn't stay there alone for a few days or so, dear." Louisa's faded eyes were serious.

"Oh, I—"

"Louisa's right, Carrie. I'll go check out the place, but I think it'd be wise if you would stay here. For tonight at least."

Carrie smiled at her friends, feeling warmth flow over her. It felt so good to have someone concerned about her. "All right. But I'll have to go back and get some of my things."

Pastor Dan clapped his hat on his head, then offered Carrie his arm. "At your service, my dear."

Carrie laughed, her heart full of love for this couple whom she loved as parents. "We'll be back in a few minutes, Louisa."

They walked the short distance to Carrie's house in companionable silence. As Carrie gathered her things, Pastor Dan took a quick peek through the house.

"Everything looks fine in here, Carrie."

"Yes. I don't think he was brave enough to come to the house." She thought for a moment. "I really don't know that it was Clarence. It could have just been a drifter trying to find a warm place to sleep."

The minister shrugged. "No telling. Are you ready to go?"

"Yes, I guess I am."

Pastor Dan struggled to keep from laughing as he reached out to take Carrie's bag. "Why on earth are you bringing this?"

Carrie glanced at the enormous family Bible she had placed on the top of her bag. She giggled. "I guess it is a bit large. But I'm. . .ah. . .without my other Bible right now, and I just can't bear not to have one to read."

Pastor Dan raised his eyebrows.

Carrie sighed. She hadn't meant to sound so woebegone. "I wasn't going to tell you because you'll just worry."

"Tell me what, please?"

"I accidentally left my Bible behind when Henry Young and I left Frank Yeakley's cabin."

"And so?"

"Sometime, I have to go get it."

"Carrie—"

"It'll be all right, Pastor Dan. I've left a message for Henry at the post office to get in touch with me the next time he comes into town. I'm sure he'll accompany me."

"Why can't he just get it for you on one of his trips up there?"

Carrie shook her head. "It's not just any Bible, Pastor. It's. . . I just have to get it myself." Her words ended on a sob, much to her chagrin.

"Why, Carrie, what's wrong, dear?" The elderly minister was distressed at her tears. "Carrie?" He ducked his head, trying to see her eyes, then suddenly the light dawned. "Ah, it's the Bible our Zach gave you, isn't it?"

She nodded, unmasked misery filling her eyes. "I can't let anything happen to it, Pastor. It's the only thing I have left. . . ."

❧

She was enjoying her visit with the Petersons, she truly was. But as several more days went by with no word from Henry, she grew increasingly restless. Finally she could stand it no longer. *What if drifters found the cabin and took the Bible? What if rats got in and chewed it up? What if. . .*

"I'm going to take Molasses out for some exercise today, Louisa. She's been getting fat and sassy without me riding her every day."

Her friend studied her from across the breakfast table. "All right, dear. Will you be back in time for dinner?"

Carrie gulped. "No, but I'll try to be back for supper. Is there anything I can pick up for you in town?"

❧

Her hands shook as she saddled Molasses. "Louisa and Pastor Dan would have my head if they knew what I was doing," she confessed to the horse. "But we'll make it, won't we, girl? I'm sure I remember the way." Whistling for Toby, she swung up into the saddle. The little dog jumped around in excitement at the prospect of an adventure.

The breeze was brisk as they headed out of town. Carrie took a huge breath of the cool air and let it out slowly. It felt good to be in the saddle again.

The trail begin to slope slightly upward as soon as she left town. She confidently turned Molasses toward the left. *It's about ten o'clock now,* she decided, squinting at the sun. *I think it took us about three hours to get there last time.* She smiled. *I should be back in plenty of time for supper.*

Two hours later, she gratefully dismounted at the same spot she and Henry had stopped almost a month ago. She laughed as Molasses and Toby eagerly drank from the icy stream. "I guess you two are as dry as I am."

His thirst quenched, Toby lay down in the dry weeds and was asleep instantly. *What a simple life,* Carrie mused. *Eat, drink, and sleep.* Yawning, she glanced up at the sky. A thick layer of ominous-looking clouds looming in the west startled her. Where had those come from?

Frowning, she gathered her things. Never before could she remember snow coming this early in the season, but from the looks of those clouds, come it would. Common sense urged her to turn back, but she argued against it. "If I don't get my Bible before the snow comes I may never get it back. We can't turn around now that we've come this far," she told Molasses firmly. She scooped up Toby and settled him in front of her on the saddle. He snuggled against her with a whooshing sigh. Once set, she nudged Molasses into a brisk pace. The terrain here was fairly smooth, with only a gradual incline. But before long, the trail grew steep and rocky. Carrie urged the panting horse on, glancing at the sky every few minutes. "I know we can beat it," she muttered.

She heaved a sigh of relief as she spotted the place where she and Henry had crossed the river. Once they forded the river, the cabin was only a stone's throw away. Surveying the half-frozen river, Carrie decided it would be safest to lead Molasses across. Somehow, it seemed to be flowing swifter than when she was here with Henry a few weeks ago. She slipped off the horse and grasped the reins tightly. They picked their way across with caution, avoiding the thickening ice. The water was only knee-deep here, but the current was even stronger than it had appeared from the bank. Carrie felt the frigid wetness soaking through her petticoats; chilling her almost instantly. Toby leapt from rock to rock, reaching the opposite bank with ease.

She glanced up at him, just in time to see an enormous piece of ice from upstream come rushing toward her. Releasing the reins, she jumped to the nearest rock, but it was too late. The ice crashed between her and Molasses, cutting a deep gash in Carrie's leg, and sending her to her knees with a scream of pain. Struggling to maintain her balance, Carrie clawed at the slippery granite slab before tumbling into the icy flow. The bitter cold snatched her breath away. *God, help me!* The prayer flashed through her mind as she fumbled for something solid. Fighting to keep her head above the current, she flung herself toward a boulder. Bracing herself against its rough solidness, she was able to push herself to a standing position. The pain in her leg brought instant tears. She clenched her jaw, willing herself to inch her way over to Molasses. The mare had regained her footing and was shivering a foot away from Carrie. Finally grasping the reins, she took a deep breath. "Come on, girl," she whispered. "Help me get across. You can do it."

Moments later Carrie lay on the bank, panting with exertion and shaking uncontrollably. She wasn't sure if it was just from the cold, or if she was going into shock. Her mind went numb, and the first gentle snowflakes began to fall, as silent as the wilderness around her.

twenty-six

Zach stood in the doorway of the tiny cabin, watching the sky. With a smile, he closed the door and turned back toward the warmth of the fireplace. Settling onto the dirt floor, he reached again for his Bible. What a wonder it had been to find it here, in Frank Yeakley's cabin. How it had gotten here, he didn't know, but he hoped that it meant that Carrie had been here. Maybe she had tended to the dying man. Just the thought of it sent a thrill through his heart. He smiled again as he tenderly stroked the smooth cover. *God must have had you leave this here just for me, Carrie.*

He recalled the first time he had walked into the cabin. Was it just yesterday? Nothing but a cold silence had greeted him, filling him with dread. Was he too late to fulfill his promise? Walking back outside, he spied the fresh mound of dirt and small marker he had failed to notice before. Remorse flooded over him as he realized he could never fulfill his vow to Clarence. It was too late. Sinking down beside the rough grave, he wept. *God, can't I do one thing right in my life?*

Daylight slipped into dusk before he knew it. Rising stiffly from the cold ground, he sighed. *Guess I'll have to spend the night here.* He grimaced at the thought of the filthy cabin. At least it would be better than being out in the cold. Maybe.

From the crispness of the air, he knew it couldn't be long before the first snow would fly. Pushing open the door of the cabin, he took a deep breath. He pulled a match from his pocket and struck it. The tiny flare lit the room for a brief moment, but it was enough time for him to spot a lantern hanging on a nail above the bed.

Unwilling to waste another match, he groped across the room, feeling for the wall. The stench that rose from the

155

bedclothes gagged him as he reached for the lamp. Gasping, he snatched the lantern and bolted for the door. Leaning his forehead against a tree, he took great gulps of fresh air.

He made his bed under the stars that night. After all, what was one more night?

☙

Morning dawned bright and clear. Zach opened one eye, reluctant to greet the dawn of another day of uncertainty. What should he do now? Frank Yeakley was dead. So was Clarence. And he, miserable wretch of a man Zach Tanner, was still alive. Why? He watched the naked aspen trees blow in the chill wind. *Just like me,* he mused. *Stripped of everything, except a tiny spark of life left inside.* Spring would come to the mountains like clockwork; the tiny leaf buds opening to a warm April sun. But when would spring come to the frozen soul of a wayward man?

Heaving a great sigh, he sat up, pulling the blanket tighter around his shoulders. Stirring up the still-glowing embers of his fire, he sat back to await the warmth. What now? Where would he go? What would he do? He had been so close to Carrie—was it just a few days ago? But still so far, somehow.

The blackness in his soul seemed to press in on him. He glanced at the grave, then at the cabin again. Why not just stay here for a while? He could live here off the land for the rest of his life, and no one would even know. Isn't that what he deserved after throwing away the life God had given him? He deserved to die a lonely, unloved man.

His decision made, he set to work with a purposeful energy. After burning the bedding and dragging every stick of furniture out of the cabin, he stood surveying the tiny room as the sunlight filtered weakly through the one inadequate window. He would wash the walls and give the floor a good sweeping; then the place would be as good as new. Ducking his head to enter the cabin, he strode over to examine the fireplace, grunting as he tripped and narrowly escaped gashing his head on the rude mantle. Regaining his balance, he scanned the floor.

What had he stepped on? As his eyes adjusted to the dim light, he saw it. Reaching down as if in a trance, he grasped the Bible and hugged it to his chest.

The improbability escaped him in the joy of the moment. His own Bible, that he had given to Carrie—it was here! It didn't matter how. It was a tangible sign that God still loved him! Why else would his very own Bible be here? Shaking like a man with the palsy, he bolted out the door and into the brightness of the clear Colorado morning. All else forgotten, he sank down onto the chopping block. He opened the precious Book to 1 John, and read the verse that Clarence had quoted to him so many months ago. Had his memory tricked him? Or would the words say what he thought they would? "If we confess our sins, he is faithful and just to forgive us our sins, and to cleanse us from all unrighteousness." He read it again and again through tear-blurred eyes. It was true. It said *all* sins.

Could he dare believe it? And after all this time? He read it again, just to be sure.

"Jesus, help me!" he cried out loud. "I want so badly to come back to You. Oh, God. Please forgive me. . . ." The dam broke as the tears of a thousand anguished nights came flowing from his soul.

Raising his head at last, he felt the peace come to him gently, like a nourishing spring rain. He took a deep breath, almost afraid to believe the joy that began to fill his heart. It had been so long since he had felt the light of Christ's love penetrate the darkness of his soul.

❧

And now, a day later, he had to wonder what God had in store for him. He was sure the Almighty hadn't forgiven him just to have him squander his life away in a remote mountain cabin. He moved to the tiny window, watching the snow begin to cover the ground. He'd better get some water before the storm really hit. He pulled on his only spare shirt before donning his coat. It was sure to get colder before he got back from his trek to the river.

Grabbing the water buckets that sat outside the door, he closed the door behind him. The smoke rising from the chimney gave him a sense of comfort as he glanced back at the tiny cabin. At least it would be warm and welcoming when he got back.

Easily covering the two miles to the river, he knelt down to dip the icy water into the first bucket. The current was strong, but still the ice had begun to form like a mirror on top of the water. Hefting the first bucket out of the water, he paused. Was that a dog barking? He straightened, glancing around. As far as he knew, no one lived within miles of here. He reached for the second bucket, tensing as he heard it again. It was a dog, no doubt about it. Dropping the bucket, he took a step in the direction of the short, distressed barks. The snow intensified, stinging his cheeks. He walked a few more feet, then stopped, trying to determine the direction the sound was coming from. The wind made it difficult to hear, but the unmistakable sound continued. Was the dog injured? Zach glanced back to where his buckets waited, then shrugged and turned once again toward the noise. He couldn't find it in his heart to leave even a dog out in this weather.

Breaking into a run, he rounded a bend in the river. A brown ball of fur hurled itself joyfully at his kneecaps, startling him. He bent down to examine the animal. "Good grief! Toby! What in the world are you doing way up here?" He couldn't believe that Carrie's little dog would be this far from home—unless she. . . "Take me to her, boy," he whispered, setting the wiggling animal on his feet.

Toby barked shrilly, making a beeline for the tree-lined bank. Zach followed, his heart in his throat. Pushing his way through the tall, snow-covered weeds, he gasped when he saw her. Was she—dead? Toby stood over her, panting. Falling to his knees, Zach pulled her cold form to his breast.

twenty-seven

Zach realized he had little time to get Carrie inside and dry or she would die of exposure. He wrapped her in his coat and gathered her cold form. He staggered under the weight of her clothes and the chill creeping through him as the wetness of her clothing began to soak into his arms. He quickly scanned both sides of the riverbank but saw no horse and no sign of anyone who might have been accompanying her.

"What was she doing up here, Toby? Were you two alone?" He shook his head at the little dog. "I can't believe I'm asking you like you're going to explain it to me." Zach heard his teeth chattering as he spoke. "Let's go, boy. It's a long hike; maybe it'll warm us up."

Zach looked at Carrie's face. She lay white and limp in his arms as he began to slowly pick his way along the trail, now slick from the fresh snow. Toby barked and turned toward the river.

"No, Toby. We're going this way."

Toby barked again and turned toward the river, his ears forward. Zach listened carefully.

"It's just the wind, boy. Come on." Zach took two more steps. *What was that?*

Toby began to bark excitedly and bounded for the riverbank.

"Toby!" Zach called after him. *Carrie would never forgive me for leaving her beloved dog behind in a snowstorm,* he chided himself, *if she lives.* "Toby! Here, boy!" Trapped by the urgent need to get Carrie inside and warm, Zach turned toward the cabin again.

There it is again. Toby bounded around the bend in the trail and back toward him, stopping just a few feet away. He barked again, turned, and ran off again. "What are you trying to tell me?" Zach called after him, indecision and cold seizing his senses. *Dear God, show me what to do,* Zach prayed. Zach's feet carried him a few steps downhill just as the head of a horse appeared around the bend in the trail. Above it Zach saw a familiar face.

"Dan?" His voice came as a strangled whisper.

Pastor Dan's eyes flew to the stranger's bearded face. "Who—what?" He looked closer. "Zach. . .is that you?"

Zach nodded, his eyes tearing. A second horse appeared bearing Sister Louisa.

The minister looked at Carrie, a look of horror gripping his face.

Zach pulled her closer. "We've got to get her out of this cold."

"Lead the way, son." Pastor Dan slid off the horse, motioning for Zach to mount. With the minister's help, Zach gently laid Carrie across the horse's neck before he mounted.

Pastor Dan mounted Louisa's horse in front of his weeping wife.

≥∙

The two men went outside to tend the horses and gather more firewood while Sister Louisa tended to the still-unconscious Carrie. After peeling off the layers of frozen clothes, she dressed Carrie in the mostly dry shirt that Zach had stripped off from under his spare shirt. She then wrapped Carrie in the lone blanket that had been warming by the fire.

Distressed that there was no bed for her patient, Louisa had stuck her head out the door and dispatched her husband to cut some pine boughs.

Zach came back in as soon as Louisa signaled to him. Shaking the snow out of his hair, he warmed his hands in front of the fire before squatting in front of Carrie. He glanced in Louisa's direction. "If you'll just keep her covered, I need to check her over. I don't know if she fell in the river, or what happened." He probed her body gently, checking for broken bones.

"She has a bad wound on her calf, Zach." Louisa pulled the

blanket away just enough to reveal the jagged cut.

He cleaned the wound as best as he could with his meager supplies, wishing for his black bag for the first time in a very long time. Finally he straightened. "I don't think it's as bad as it looks. Our main problem will be keeping her warm enough." He shook his head. "It will be a miracle if she doesn't get pneumonia."

"Seems like God is in the miracle-working business," Louisa said softly.

Zach jerked around to look at her, meeting her eyes for the first time. "Guess you're right," he said. A pensive expression crossed his face, then he smiled. "It's a good thing He is."

Louisa nodded, her smile telling him that her heart was too full for words.

❧

Carrie lay snug on her pine-bough bed in front of the fire; the three others gathered around closely, two chairs and two saddles their only seating. Toby snored softly, sprawled across Zach's feet. "God's Word says that if there's any sick among you, to call for the elders of the church and to anoint the sick with oil and pray for them and they will be healed," Pastor Dan said. "I believe that we could act on that verse, don't you?"

Substituting a bit of bear grease for oil, the minister gently stroked Carrie's forehead, then laid his hand on her shoulder. The others followed suit. Silence descended for a long moment before Pastor Dan began to pray quietly. "Father God, thank You for sparing Carrie's life today. Thank You for sending Zach to find her and for using us to help him. Thank You for Your unfailing kindness to us. God, in Your Word it says that the prayer of faith shall save the sick. Now, God, Carrie is Your child. . . ."

Zach kept his eyes closed, but the tears flooded down his cheeks anyway. How little he deserved the privilege to approach God in prayer—to ask anything of such a holy, righteous Father. But because of Jesus—because of Jesus' cleansing blood that was shed on Calvary—he, Zach Tanner, could come boldly to the throne of grace—to find grace and mercy in the time of need. His hand trembled on Carrie's forehead as a great wave of thanksgiving rolled through his soul. Forgetting that anyone else was in the room, he suddenly broke forth into shouts of praise. The sheer joy of forgiveness and grace caused him to want to jump up and down. Lifting his hands heavenward, he shouted his praise to God. And Carrie never stirred.

❧

Pastor Dan and Sister Louisa sat staring at Zach in amazement as he told them the story of his last three years. "It's still hard to believe that Clarence would. . .do what he did for me," Zach said.

"Amazing." Pastor Dan tented his fingers. "You've been given a precious gift, Zach. Not many people get a second chance at life."

"I know. I just don't know what He wants of me yet."

The elderly minister glanced at Carrie. "I'm assuming you want Carrie to be a part of it?"

Zach made no attempt to hide the sudden moisture in his eyes. "More than anything. But after what I did to her—"

"She'll forgive you, son."

"How can you be so sure?" He brushed a hand across his eyes.

"Because she loves you."

Zach studied Carrie's still face. "How could she?" he whispered.

"She would have to be the one to tell you that, son," Dan said. "But I hope it can wait until morning, because we all need to get some sleep."

Zach glanced at Louisa's nodding figure. "Looks like some of us have already figured that out."

❧

A chorus of snores soon filled the small room as Pastor Dan and Sister Louisa reclined against their saddles. Zach picked up the Bible, inching closer to Carrie until he was close enough to touch her. He would watch her through the night.

Taking her work-roughened hand in his, he listened to her regular breathing. He tenderly stroked her hair back from her forehead, the coppery strands feeling like silk as they slipped through his fingers. He thought back again on the last few hours, marveling at the way events had unfolded. Who would have thought that today he would have a chance to hold her in his arms? The desire to kiss her made him ache with longing, threatening to dispel whatever good judgment he possessed. But he would not take advantage of her.

He traced her features with his eyes. Maybe she didn't even want him anymore. Pastor Dan had as much as promised that she still loved him, but he'd have to hear it from her own lips and read it in her eyes before he would believe it. He sighed, pressing her hand to his chest.

Hours later, he felt her eyes on him as he dozed. Raising his head, he lost himself in her gaze.

"Is it really you, Zach?" she whispered. Her voice was hoarse.

He squeezed her hand that he still held close to his heart. "It's really me."

They stared at each other for another long moment. He watched her eyes fall on their clasped hands, then move back up to his face. "How did you find me?"

Not trusting his voice, Zach pointed heavenward.

She nodded. "I knew He would send someone." She coughed, grimacing at the pain in her throat. Laying her head back down, her eyes slipped closed only to open again a minute later. She searched Zach's face as if trying to know his thoughts. "Would you. . .kiss me?"

His heart had begun pounding wildly the moment she had opened her eyes; now it seemed to stop. He cupped her face in his hands, lowering his face toward hers. He heard her catch her breath, then his lips found hers.

The kiss was achingly sweet, filled with all the longing of

the past and all the hope of the future. When he at last lifted his face, he saw the tears that had filled her eyes. "Ah, Carrie. I've finally come home."

She wiped at the tears that had trickled down her face, then lifted her still-damp palm to his cheek. "I've missed you so much." Her voice cracked then, and she smiled sleepily.

He pressed his hand gently over her eyes. "Go back to sleep now. I'll be right here."

twenty-eight

She still loves me! He had seen it in her eyes and felt it in her kiss. Zach felt like running around and shouting his joy to the world, but it was still the middle of the night. He grasped the Bible once again, willing himself to sit down. There would be time enough for celebration in the morning.

He gazed at Carrie tenderly, replaying the last few minutes in his mind. She loved him! How could that be? Would she still love him after she knew all the rotten things he had done? He frowned. Maybe he shouldn't tell her.

But he had to. There would be no more secrets between them. He would tell her everything. After all, God had forgiven him of those things. He wasn't the same Zach Tanner she knew so long ago, but then he doubted she was the same, either.

He smiled, thinking of all the catching up they had to do. Balancing the old Bible on his knees, he studied it in the dim light of the fire. Who would have thought that this would be the instrument that brought him back to life? He laid his head down on the cool leather, suddenly tired. Hours later, he jumped as the Bible fell to the floor. He must have fallen asleep.

The first rays of light were finding their way through the dusty window as he reached to retrieve the Bible. A lone sheet of paper had fallen out. Intending to replace it, he picked it up. Wrinkled and water-stained, the letter looked like it had been read many times.

It really was none of his business, but—he froze as he read the last lines. *It won't be long until we can be together always. All my love, Philip.* He dropped the letter as if it were burning his hand. *Oh, dear God. Surely not. Surely she hasn't found someone else. . . .*

He bolted out the door. The frigid wind slammed him in the

face, but he pressed on. Not stopping until he reached the river, he huddled under an enormous conifer. "God!" he called out loud. "Why did You do this to me? I thought You brought me to her. . . ." Racking sobs burst from his lips, the hot tears melting the snowflakes that clung to his face. "I don't think I can live without her!"

If only he hadn't seen her. . .touched her. . .kissed her. He could have stood it if he had stayed away. But now to be so close—he sank down to the freezing ground, his head in his hands. *But she loves me. I know she does. I felt it when I kissed her. Unless she thought she was kissing someone else.* The thought chilled him more than the arctic wind. He thought once again of the tender kiss they had shared. Maybe she had been delirious—or still asleep. . . .

His tormenting thoughts drove him back to his feet. He would just leave; get out of her life forever. The sooner the better for both of them. Without a backward glance, he started upriver. Where, he didn't know. Did it really matter?

Only when he was too exhausted to push himself farther did he yield to the still, small voice that tugged at his soul. *And will you forsake Me again, too?* Dropping to his knees in the deepening snow, he bowed his head. Would he? Could he turn his back on God again? His only hope in the world?

The snow had begun to collect on his eyelashes before he could still the agony of his soul enough to think. He was a little boy again, sitting on his father's lap. "Many of Jesus' followers turned away from Him that day," Papa had said. "Then Jesus turned and asked His disciples, 'Will you leave me, too?' And Peter said, 'Lord, where would we go? You are the truth.' "

Zach wept bitterly. Where would he go? He already knew the truth. "God, why are You asking so much of me?" he cried. "You know I don't want to turn my back on You again, but why must You give me such a heavy cross to bear?"

Silence.

Zach stared at the sky for long minutes, ignoring the falling snow. He knew the war raging in his soul would end either one way or the other—life or death. And spiritual death was worse by far than physical death. The last three years had convinced him of that.

Would you, too, forsake Me? No. No! He could not walk away from his Savior again. He jumped to his feet, feeling the conviction rising in his soul. Nothing God would ask of him would be too much. "I will serve You, Father. Even in this, I submit myself to You."

The only answer was the deep, rock-solid peace that comes from total surrender to God.

The soft whinny nudged him back to the cold, snowy world beside the riverbank. Glancing up, he saw Molasses, her reins entangled in the gnarled branches of a fallen spruce tree.

Commanding his half-frozen legs to move, he tottered over to where the horse stood. "Molasses. Thank God!" He had been a fool to run out into this foul weather in only his shirt-sleeves. But once again, God provided a way of escape.

His numb fingers could scarcely feel the smooth leather of the reins as he fought to unwind them from the rough branches. He stopped and blew on his hands, then tried one last time. Success at last! Drawing on sheer willpower, he hoisted himself up into the saddle. Hunching over to shield his face from the biting wind, he guided the mare back toward the cabin.

Surely Carrie would have awakened by now. A sad smile tugged at his lips. He would return Molasses, get warmed up, and then leave. No use prolonging the agony.

Pastor Dan met him half a mile from the cabin, looking like a walking snowman. "Zach! Where have you been? The women have been worried sick!"

Zach leaned over to look at the minister and nearly slipped from the saddle. "Have to go." His words barely escaped through his frozen lips.

"What?" Grasping the reins, Pastor Dan led the way back to the cabin in silence.

It was only until Zach was thawing by the fire that he dared look at Carrie. The questions in her eyes were so arresting that he had to turn away. "Guess I'll be on my way as soon as my clothes dry out."

Three sets of eyes turned to stare at him.

"On your way where, Zach?"

The question hung in the air for a long minute. He shrugged. "Back home, I guess." Home? Where was that?

Carrie gave a strangled little cry. "Zach, I thought. . ." Her voice broke and she hid her face in her hands.

Despite his pain, Zach felt the anger rise in his breast. *How could she act like that, when she. . .?* "Why should it matter to you where I go?" he asked, his voice louder than he had intended.

Louisa glared at him. "Don't you talk to Carrie that way, Zach. She—"

"Zach. When we talked last night, you said that you wanted Carrie to—"

Zach jumped to his feet, interrupting the minister. "That was before I found the letter."

He felt the weight of Carrie's gaze again.

"What are you talking about, Zach?"

He squinted at her. "You don't have to pretend, Carrie. I saw the letter from him—from Philip."

"A letter from Phil—" Her wrinkled brow was suddenly smoothed. "If that's all the problem is. . . ." She rose stiffly and pulled the Bible from the mantle. "Do you mean this letter?"

Zach grimaced as she held up the hateful paper.

She handed it to him. "Read it, Zach."

"Why?" He grasped it gingerly as if it might bite his hand off.

Pastor Dan rolled his eyes. "Just do as she says, Zach, for goodness' sake."

Zach glanced at his friend, then lowered his eyes to the letter. Halfway through, he felt the warmth rise to his cheeks.

What an idiot he had been to go off half-cocked. Even though the first page was missing, he realized that this letter wasn't even Carrie's. It was Annabelle's.

He looked up to find her gaze on him, her heart in her eyes.

"I don't know what to say, Carrie." He stepped over to her, taking her hands in his. "Actually, it seems that there's a lot I should say."

She smiled then, making his heart turn over. "You don't have to say anything," she whispered. "Just kiss me like you did last night, and I'll know everything is all right."

Pastor Dan cleared his throat. "It looks as if the snow has finally stopped. Would you care to take a stroll outside, Louisa dear?"

She beamed up at him. "Certainly. Just let me get my hat."

epilogue

"Well, Mrs. Tanner, what do you think of our land?"

The newlyweds stood on the bank, listening once again to the music of the waterfall.

Carrie glanced up at her husband, not sure she had heard him correctly. "Our land?"

Zach nodded. "Remember the infamous night that Clarence and I had it out? I had just been over at Mr. Parker's house, concluding the deal."

The last piece of the puzzle fell together for Carrie. "All of this is ours?"

"Mama had some money put away for me. She said I could use it any way I wanted, as long as it would help the cause of Christ. And so I thought that we could build a clinic—"

"And have some of the girls from the orphanage come and train here!"

He hugged her to him, chuckling. "My idea exactly."

"Of course it was, Zach. We're one now, remember?"

"Flesh of my flesh; bone of my bone," he murmured, leading her gently to the sun-warmed bank. A cluster of sky-blue columbines caught his eye, and he smiled. The flowers of life might fade, but the Word of the Lord would indeed endure forever.

A Letter To Our Readers

Dear Reader:

In order that we might better contribute to your reading enjoyment, we would appreciate your taking a few minutes to respond to the following questions. We welcome your comments and read each form and letter we receive. When completed, please return to the following:

Rebecca Germany, Fiction Editor
Heartsong Presents
PO Box 719
Uhrichsville, Ohio 44683

1. Did you enjoy reading *After the Flowers Fade?*
   ☐ Very much. I would like to see more books by this author!
   ☐ Moderately
   I would have enjoyed it more if _____

   _____

   _____

2. Are you a member of **Heartsong Presents**? Yes ☐ No ☐
   If no, where did you purchase this book? _____

   _____

3. How would you rate, on a scale from 1 (poor) to 5 (superior), the cover design? _____

4. On a scale from 1 (poor) to 10 (superior), please rate the following elements.

   _____ Heroine   _____ Plot

   _____ Hero   _____ Inspirational theme

   _____ Setting   _____ Secondary characters

5. These characters were special because_____

   _____

   _____

6. How has this book inspired your life?_____

   _____

   _____

7. What settings would you like to see covered in future
   Heartsong Presents books?_____

   _____

   _____

8. What are some inspirational themes you would like to see
   treated in future books?_____

   _____

   _____

9. Would you be interested in reading other **Heartsong
   Presents** titles?   Yes ❑   No ❑

10. Please check your age range:
    ❑ Under 18   ❑ 18-24   ❑ 25-34
    ❑ 35-45   ❑ 46-55   ❑ Over 55

11. How many hours per week do you read?_____

Name _____

Occupation _____

Address _____

City _____ State _____ Zip _____

Relax this Christmas

And enjoy the Christmas Season with our two new novella collections—*Fireside Christmas* and *Winter Wishes*—both have four new stories in one big volume for only $7.94 for the pair.

Experience love stories from days gone by in ***Fireside Christmas*** as Kristin Billerbeck, Peggy Darty, Rosey Dow, and JoAnn A. Grote take you back to simpler times.

Brand-new stories from today abound with love and charm in ***Winter Wishes*** when you curl up with Yvonne Lehman, Loree Lough, Colleen L. Reece, and Debra White Smith as they tell you about modern day romances.

♥ ♥ ♥ ♥ ♥ ♥ **♥** ♥ ♥ ♥ ♥ ♥ ♥

Please send me _____ copies of *Fireside Christmas* and _____ copies of *Winter Wishes*. I am enclosing $4.97 each. Or send me _____ set(s) for $7.94.
(Please add $1.00 to cover postage and handling per order. OH add 6% tax.)
Send check or money order, no cash or C.O.D.s please.

Name_____

Address _____

City, State, Zip _____

To place a credit card order, call 1-800-847-8270.
Send to: Heartsong Presents Reader Service, PO Box 719, Uhrichsville, OH 44683

♥ ♥ ♥ ♥ ♥ ♥ **♥** ♥ ♥ ♥ ♥ ♥ ♥

·········Presents·········

Great Inspirational Romance at a Great Price!

Heartsong Presents books are inspirational romances in contemporary and historical settings, designed to give you an enjoyable, spirit-lifting reading experience. You can choose wonderfully written titles from some of today's best authors like Peggy Darty, Sally Laity, Tracie Peterson, Colleen L. Reece, Lauraine Snelling, and many others.

When ordering quantities less than twelve, above titles are $2.95 each.
Not all titles may be available at time of order.